THE
BROOKWOOD
BOYS

Patrick Larsimont

SAPERE
BOOKS

THE
BROOKWOOD
BOYS

Published by Sapere Books.

24 Trafalgar Road, Ilkley, LS29 8HH

saperebooks.com

ISBN: 978-0-85495-525-1

For my wife Alison and my dear friend Kari, who on a walk around Brookwood Cemetery pushed me to write this story. Dedicated also to the men and women buried and commemorated at Brookwood. Your stories are my inspiration.

CHAPTER ONE

Brookwood Military Cemetery, England, 2019

Dawn has always been my favourite time of day. I take my tour of Brookwood Cemetery nearly every morning, at sun-up. Starting at the main gate, I walk the avenue of red pines rising up on either side of the black tar road leading out of the cemetery gates. Sweet-smelling in the morning, the pines remind me of my home in Tennessee. I can recall when they were planted here, carefully, protected by fencing on account of being rare. They're huge now and when the wind blows, they shriek and groan, giving visitors a fright as they sway.

Off the avenue, rows of headstones stretch as far as the eye can see. This morning, the skirl of the bagpipes tells me that old Canuck Jack Benzie is playing his 'Flowers of the Forest' again. Spread amongst the rows, I can see familiar faces and I greet them with a hearty 'good morning'. Some are quite distinct, others fainter, mere shadows of what they once were.

I pass by the memorials at the inner gates. There's always something new getting built around here. It can get confusing, but I suppose anything that keeps people thinking about us old boys can't be a bad thing. We had a real nice memorial carved from creamy sandstone just opposite the Canadian plot, but it went green, so they replaced it with something a bit more hardy. It commemorates 308 British and Commonwealth soldiers who died with no known grave during World War One.

There's an even bigger one, called the Brookwood Memorial to the Missing, which honours the 3,428 soldiers, men and women from the Commonwealth, who died lost and unknown during World War Two. I'm being specific about the numbers because I reckon it's important to get it right. Maybe that's on account of my own cross having no name. *I know I'm here,* but no one else does.

The American Military Cemetery where I'm buried was donated to the American people in 1918. At the war's end, all the American troops who died across the country were gathered up here. There are rows of white marble crosses in four plots clustered around the Stars and Stripes. A sandstone chapel stands to the north, with stained glass that casts coloured reflections across the altar, furled flags and a large stone cross. Outside on the lawn are the crosses of forty-one unknown warriors. I am one of them.

The epitaph on my grave reads:

> *HERE RESTS IN HONORED GLORY*
> *AN AMERICAN SOLDIER*
> *KNOWN BUT TO GOD*

But they knew my name. They just didn't want the first American boy buried in their fancy cemetery to be a Black man.

I'm Sergeant Maurice Forsyth from Memphis, Tennessee. People call me Mouse, on account of being born kind of small. The name stuck with me all of my life, and followed me for the last hundred years since I got myself killed. I was born in 1878, slap bang in the middle of a yellow fever epidemic, which took both my parents and sister before I was even one. It was my Uncle Red who brought me up on his mule farm. He wasn't such a bad man, just kind of rough and not too smart. He went and got himself killed when I was just eighteen. I was on my own after that, keeping myself to myself, learning my letters and the joy of reading. I spent near enough twenty years on the road, running mule trains up and down from Memphis and hauling cotton from plantations across Mississippi, Arkansas and Tennessee.

I was nearly forty when war in Europe changed everything for me. The British had run out of horses after the slaughter of France and Gallipoli. They'd searched their empire for horseflesh; wild bush ponies from Australia called Brumbies and huge donkeys from the deserts of Egypt, but it was good old-fashioned American mules that saved the day. In 1916, an ordinary pack mule was worth $175. By the time I left for Europe, it was worth over $230. That's a thirty percent increase. I was suddenly sitting on a goldmine.

Right about then, a government fellow came to me. 'The US Army needs men with your know-how,' he said. Well, I knew nothing about soldiering, but this gentleman told me he was going to pay me a whole lot of money, give me some stripes in the US Army, and put me in charge of a bunch of ornery mules and an even meaner bunch of muleskinners. I got a fine uniform, with good boots, gaiters and riding britches, a jacket that buttoned up at the collar, and sergeant stripes on my arms and a horseshoe badge on my sleeve. They gave me a big overcoat too, and a wide-brimmed hat like a Canadian Mountie. Boy, did I look fine.

My job, along with a handful of other muleskinners, was to collect three thousand beasts from right across the south. These weren't just any old mules. The British were real particular about what they wanted. They needed wheel mules: big beasts that would be closest to the heavy equipment. They had to stand fifteen hands tall and weigh at least a thousand pounds. Lead draft mules, harnessed ahead of the wheel mules, could be smaller, and regular pack mules were smaller still. Darker coloured animals were preferred, since pale ones attracted enemy fire, but I fixed that pretty quick by dyeing the lighter ones with potassium permanganate.

We shipped the herd down to New Orleans, then up the east coast in a steamer until we got to Hoboken, New Jersey. There, we were given time to shake off the seasickness and to treat the colic amongst the beasts. We bought fresh fodder, scrubbed down the mules and loaded them onto a big old ship called the SS *Leysian*, which was taking us across the ocean to Liverpool, England.

I was finally seeing the world, getting paid and fed, and all for working my mules. The men understood I knew my business, so deferred to my knowledge of the animals and their ways. Some of the Southern boys didn't much appreciate a Black man with stripes, but we soon found ourselves an understanding. The further away we got from home and the closer to war, the less those kinda things seemed to matter.

In Liverpool, we muleskinners, or what the British called muleteers, spent a week getting the beasts ready for the next stage of the journey. We handed our charges over to the British Army and got orders to head to a camp called Morn Hill, near a town called Winchester. The folks there were real friendly to American doughboys. We visited the ancient sites, and the rolling valleys called the Hampshire Downs. It was a fine time, as we waited for more shipments from the States, all part of General Pershing's build-up of troops in England. The work wasn't hard, and life was pretty good, except when some of the boys started arriving sick from Fort Riley, Kansas, after crossing the wild Atlantic.

Right about then I met my Nancy. She was a real sweet girl, whose momma was the landlady of the Old Market Inn. I was kinda surprised when this itsy-bitsy girl came up to me with mischief in those sparkling green eyes and said, 'What can I get you, handsome?'

Her momma was happy to serve Black boys, but in a separate room to avoid trouble with the white troops. Trouble still came, mind, cos them fellers didn't like us messing with English girls. My little Nancy sure loved to dance with me, though. I didn't care for it much myself, but anything that let me hold her was just fine by me.

I was probably too old for her, but she seemed to like me and I don't suppose I'm too bad looking. From being a sickly child, I grew tall and strong, and have been told I've got kind eyes and a friendly smile for them that deserves it. Nancy fell for me, and I felt the same, but I was worried that we were too different to make it work, so I called things off. I had to leave for France, and I fear I may have broken my darling's heart because she was desperate to see me before I left, but I didn't let her. That's something that still makes me sad. I never did get the chance to tell her how I truly felt. My little Nancy sure was very special to me.

My mule train was sent to join the 369th from Harlem. We left Plymouth with 450 animals and 50 muleskinners bound for Brest in Brittany. By summertime, we were in the Champagne-Marne region of France. Our job was to haul ammunition and vittles for the French 16th Division as they prepared for battle. That was when I saw what shellfire could do to men and animals for the first time. Gunners, stripped and sweating like stokers, kept up a terrible barrage of destruction. In return, the enemy's fire took a fearsome toll.

Mercifully, at that time of year, the trenches were dry, but it was easy to get lost, not something I'd recommend when leading a long line of stubborn mules. That's when a 'Bell

Sharp', a wise old mare, is key. She wears a bell so the rest can hear where she's at. I had me a fine old gal called Emmeline. Wise and clever, she kept the others calm, as long as I gave her a loaf of bread and a beer once in a while and tickled her long furry ears.

We were part of General LeBouc's 161st Division, for the summer counterattack known as the Aisne-Marne Offensive. On 25th September 1918, we advanced to support General Pershing's drive on the Meuse-Argonne. We were ordered to take the village of Séchault, but had to pull back as the enemy had brought up artillery and poison gas. Now, it weren't the first time that gas was used, but it was for me and my mules. As the gas came on, all I could do was to let them all loose and hope they might outrun the poison.

My best gal, Emmeline, was caught, her hooves pawing at the air as she suffocated. I don't mind saying I sobbed as she lay dying in my arms. She brayed pitifully for my help and those cries broke my heart right there. Something clicked deep inside. I was so furious at German cruelty and our own stupidity for failing these poor animals who had done nothing but serve us faithfully. In my blind fury, I raged until I too was overcome. My eyes started to burn, and I couldn't breathe.

Over the next three days, the regiment lost over 800 men. I don't suppose anybody bothered to count up the mules. I was one of the casualties, but I didn't die straight away. I don't remember too much about being sent back to England, to a hospital for gas casualties, but I know I finally passed somewhere in England in October 1918, just one month before the end of the war.

Waking up in an open field was terrifying at first. It took me a long time to figure out where I was, and that I was no longer alive. But it was also somehow soothing after the agony I'd endured. I felt easy and peaceful for a spell, but lonely, and I really appreciated it when others started to appear.

I was buried alongside four other fellers, 'Soldiers Known But To God'. I don't know why, but I was the only one of them to tarry. I would have appreciated a chance to talk to them boys. I've discussed it a lot with the other guys throughout the years and we can't quite figure out why some stick around and others don't. Personally, I believe if you are upset or worried when you pass, you're gonna stick. I'm not exactly sure why I did, but for me, I reckon it's down to my mules. I was real mad about my poor critters, especially my old gal Emmeline. I believe it wounded my soul.

Those of us stuck here suffer no hunger or thirst, or pain from our wounds. We simply endure the passage of time, listening and observing but unable to speak with the living. The occasional discovery of more brothers, or sisters, who have joined our vigil, provides us with some distraction, but other than that our days are much the same, and this has been my existence now for over a hundred years. I was gassed in France, just after my fortieth birthday, died and was buried near enough a month later. It is the boredom I struggle with most.

I long for something to happen, something to give me a purpose.

CHAPTER TWO

Everything changed for me one morning in April. The head gardener at Brookwood, Thomas, was working in the flowerbeds with his teenage son, Luke. They were singing along to the radio; Luke has a particularly powerful voice. I like to listen to the radio when they bring it and find the modern songs really jolly. It's just about the only way I can learn what's going on in the world. Visitors tend to keep quiet on account of this being a cemetery and all, but the radio brings the news.

Thomas doesn't talk much, except to his son. I move closer to listen in on their conversation, but when I get there, Luke is singing along to the song on the radio again. I lean over, trying to read the inscription on the headstone he's working on. It's for a boy from Newfoundland, drowned when his troopship got sunk by a U-boat up in Scotland.

I watch Luke scrub the boy's sandstone grave, wondering how many years might separate them in age, when Luke steps back and passes straight through me. I can sense a brief warmth, which in itself is unusual since we don't feel the elements, then the flutter of his heartbeat.

'Phew, what's that smell?' he asks. 'Stinks like horses.'

'Horses, Luke?' replies his father. 'There are no horses allowed here, son. You know that. It would be disrespectful. The Brookwood Boys wouldn't like it.'

Now, that's a new one on me — The Brookwood Boys. I kinda like it.

Luke closes his eyes and murmurs, 'No, not the Brookwood Boys. This one's a horse boy.' He turns and looks right at me. His eyes are glazed. 'Hello there, horse boy.'

Well, I'll be God-damned!

I stare, wide-eyed. Luke can see me, or at least sense me. What did he say? Horse boy? What else am I gonna smell of but my stinking old mules? After a hundred years of being invisible to the living, has someone finally realised I'm here? My dead old heart is soaring; in all these long and weary years, this has never happened before.

Luke is rubbing his head and his eyes seem to refocus again. He frowns; he's no longer looking in my direction. I start talking to him, then hollering to try and get his attention, but the moment has passed. I know I wasn't imagining it, though. We definitely connected.

I quickly make my way to the RAF Memorial Shelter. Taddy has to hear my news. Taddy is my closest pal here. His full name is Tadeusz Witold Lubelski. Before the war, he was destined to become a Catholic priest, so he knows a bunch about death and the afterlife. I find him sitting on a gravestone, chin on his fist, a passable double for that Rodin's 'Thinker'.

Before I can tell him my news, he says, 'She's been crying again, Mouse. It breaks my heart to see her upset like this. I hate that I can do nothing to help.'

I know exactly who he's talking about. Tilly comes up here often. We ain't quite sure who she's visiting, but she always comes alone.

'She's really upset this time, Mouse,' says Taddy. 'I followed her while she was searching the fence line, combing through rhododendrons like she'd lost something. Whatever could she be looking for?'

I sit on the damp grass beside him. Each of us has our own particular aura, linked to our death, and Taddy smells of burnt rubber, charred metal, and sickly-sweet aviation fuel. It's not the worst of the smells around here, but it's mighty powerful. Taddy was destined to be a man of peace, not war. He's an educated man, who speaks several languages. His path had been mapped out from birth. The youngest of six, his childhood was a succession of church services, choir practices, altar boy duties and a strict religious education from stern-faced priests, but he has an adventurous heart, loves opera and has a fine singing voice.

The only indulgences from his wealthy industrialist father were flying lessons for his twenty-first birthday, the proviso being he'd knuckle down at the seminary afterwards. Against his father's better judgement, he was allowed to apply to the Polish Air Force Academy at Dęblin. The odds were against him with over six thousand applicants for only ninety places, but somehow, he secured a place in the class of 1937.

In 1938, Germany annexed Czechoslovakian Sudetenland. When it then proceeded to occupy the rest of the country, Poland mobilised for war. All training intensified and any plans for the seminary flew straight out the window. Taddy earned his wings in the summer of 1939, in glorious flying weather that belied the gathering storm clouds of war.

Polish pilot wings are called *gapa* and consist of a silver eagle holding a laurel wreath in its beak. When he was awarded his, Taddy was assigned to the 132nd Fighter Escadrille, near Poznan, for training on the all-metal P.11 fighter, with a powerful radial engine and open cockpit. Despite being obsolete and outclassed by the enemy's Messerschmitt Bf 109, it possessed manoeuvrability and great visibility and it could take a lot of damage.

Taddy's first combat mission was a disaster. He developed engine problems, which forced an early return. Goggles covered in oil, the cockpit full of choking smoke, he returned to base sick and spluttering. Upon landing, he was accused of ineptitude and there were insinuations of combat shyness. Furious and determined to restore his reputation, he flew off recklessly and threw himself at a flight of Ju 87 Stuka dive bombers, which were swooping over friendly tanks on the Polish plains. The wail of the Stukas' sirens through the leather of his flight helmet were terrifying, but he was fortunate to catch one as it pulled out of a dive. A quick burst silenced the rear gunner, but not before he took several hits to his own engine. Taddy flipped the tough little aircraft over, easily matching the Stuka's evasive manoeuvres, before firing again. The result was the explosive loss of the Stuka's wing. With blood roaring in his ears, Taddy felt immediate satisfaction that he'd avenged at least some of his martyred countrymen but was then sick with remorse at having taken two lives.

The next day, Taddy was ordered to Romania, as the Polish air force scrambled to escape German ground forces overrunning one airfield after the next. After a tortuous journey across Europe, he ended up in France, catching up with other Poles serving with 1/145 *Groupe de Chasse Polonais*. Flying outdated Caudron C.714s, they managed twelve victories as *Blitzkrieg* now struck France.

Taddy's first fighter kill was a twin-engine Bf 110 *Zerstörer* with a two-man crew. Armed with 20mm cannons, four machine guns at the front and a MG 15 to the rear, it was a beast of an aircraft, twelve metres to the C.714's eight, with twice the wingspan and three times the weight. When Taddy made his first pass, he immediately rolled away to avoid the rear gunner's retaliation. He'd learnt the lesson from his Stuka, and this time was fortunate as one of the Bf 110's engines began to smoke, leaving a white trail across the sky over Dreux airfield, west of Paris. His engine seizing, the enemy sought the refuge of the clouds, but the smoke made him too obvious to lose. Taddy's beam attack startled the hiding enemy crew, as he aimed for the big black cross on its fishlike tail. A sudden boom echoed across the valley floor and the tail spun off. The rest of the aircraft spun like a sycamore seed, fuel leaking onto hot engines which burst into a brilliant halo of flame.

That was Taddy's last flight of the battle for France. The very next day, he and others were evacuated by car to La Rochelle, to catch a cargo ship bound for England. Taddy was one of thirteen pilots providing the backbone of a new Polish No. 302 Fighter Squadron. He was delighted to discover that it was to be named for his hometown of Poznan.

As the Battle of Britain gathered pace, No. 302 Squadron converted to Hawker Hurricane fighters, and moved to RAF Duxford, to become part of 12 Group's 'Big Wing'. Far from London, they saw less action than those stationed further south, but it did allow them sufficient time to gain height before engaging the enemy over the city.

Taddy was only twenty-four, a Flying Officer in the RAF Volunteer Reserve, with three victories to his name. It was an exhilarating and terrifying time, and to top it all off, he also fell in love. Good-looking, well-built, and always immaculately turned out, he made quite an impression on the ladies. The Women's Auxiliary Air Force had been drafted in as English teachers to help the Polish pilots, and that was how Taddy met his Betty. She was a Yorkshire lass from Hull, but her mother was a refugee from the Cossack pogroms and Betty had been taught by her to speak fluent Polish.

It was a whirlwind romance lived with the typical intensity of war. Nights were spent in each other's arms as the bombers droned overhead, and during the day he was on 'standby' or out on terrifying 'scrambles', meeting enemy formations targeting the cities.

With three kills to his name, Taddy needed two more to become an ace. His fourth was on what came to be known as Battle of Britain Day. The squadron scrambled from RAF Duxford, joining a 'Big Wing' formation to meet the huge air armada of enemy bombers and their escorts. He singled out a target, a Dornier 17 *Schnellbomber*, capable of outrunning any fighter, but fortunately it was hemmed in by flying in a defensive formation. Taddy's flight burst through the clouds as sunlight glinted on the bombers' cockpits, shimmering ahead of them like trout in a clear mountain stream. Taddy's eight .303 guns held three hundred rounds apiece, theoretically more than capable of bringing the Dornier down.

He carefully lined up his reflector sight, then fired a first short burst. Red defensive tracers rose to meet him, twinkling past his cork-screwing Hurricane. His rounds sparkled as they struck the bomber's canopy, shattering its translucent nose, which then dropped open like the gaping mouth of a great fish. Oxygenated air fanned the flames raging inside into an inferno and the bomber began to drop. A single parachute opened out of a crew of four — probably the rear gunner that had been firing so vigorously moments earlier. The man floated silently to earth through the mass of snarling aircraft.

After landing to refuel, Taddy spotted a solo Spitfire in trouble. It was trailing smoke and being pursued by an aggressive enemy interceptor. Taddy took off and swooped onto the unsuspecting Snapper out of the brightness of the sun, firing as soon as he was tucked in behind him. He took great care to avoid firing through the enemy onto the Spitfire that was beyond. Taddy's burst hit the Bf 109 with shuddering impacts, but its pilot pulled up and away, very skilfully. Taddy was struggling to keep on his tail and noted the kill tallies on his opponent's rudder. He was clearly an experienced ace, a proven *Experte*.

The metallic taste of fear rose in Taddy's mouth as he pressed his Hurricane into the desperate pursuit. Glancing sideways, he saw the ailing Spitfire make good its escape, while its aggressor was otherwise engaged. The ace twisted and turned, but Taddy grimly held on, grateful his opening burst had winged him. He recognised the thin white trail of a coolant leak, realising his opponent's engine would be overheating and likely to seize up when the trailing smoke turned black.

In a desperate final manoeuvre, the ace rolled and attempted an Immelmann loop to gain altitude and then bring his guns to bear. His dying engine lacked the power, and the anticipated black smoke traced the manoeuvre, making it visible and obvious. A more inexperienced pilot might have sheared off when confronted by the sight of an aggressive enemy swooping at him head-on, but at Dęblin, Taddy had been taught to fire through frontal attacks.

The Bf 109 roared towards the Hurricane, expecting it to pull away and so over-shoot, but Taddy fired straight and deep into the yellow cowling to reach the black heart of the failing engine. The ace's aircraft reared up like a bucking horse, then fell like a stone. Taddy had to bank to see it slam into the mudflats off Leigh-on-Sea in Essex. He couldn't believe he'd escaped unharmed, and he laughed with nervous relief. It then dawned on him; he was finally an ace.

Taddy was the hero of the hour. Betty's relief was palpable, leading to happy tears after a few drinks. Taddy had never seen someone care for him so deeply and he asked for her hand in marriage. Both now in tears, they were carried shoulder-high by cheering friends and comrades. In lieu of an engagement ring, Taddy fashioned a brooch from his spare *gapa* wings for Betty to wear.

But his happiness turned to tragedy on the 18th of September, 1940. Determined to assert his new status as an ace, Taddy flew aggressively from the outset, when his squadron approached a formation of Ju 88s. Swooping down with Red Section, he lined up the lead bomber, when he was hit hard from behind by the next Ju 88 in their boxed formation. A bright magnesium flash was followed by a sharp detonation, and several red streaks flew past his cockpit from astern. He smelt something chemical. Cordite? Phosphorous? He couldn't tell.

The Hurricane is a tough old bird, but not if the instrument panel is shattered and shot through. He first smelt, then saw aviation fuel sloshing around his feet. It ignited with an ominous crump, flames swiftly enveloping his flight boots. Panic coursed through him as he tugged at the canopy. The stench of burning filled his nostrils as an eerie calm descended upon him. Images of Betty's face that gave him strength were interrupted, as searing pain reached his exposed hands and face.

The canopy mercifully lurched back, and he was free. Tipping out of the inverted Hurricane, his mask was ripped away from his face. Completely disorientated, cold air stung his burns as he struggled to find the parachute cord. With the ground hurtling towards him, his blackened fingers searched for the handle, finding it at last and giving it a desperate tug. He was jerked skywards, groaning as the straps bit into his burns. As he fell, he beat his legs together, trying to extinguish the flames that were licking up his flying suit.

Barely conscious, he landed in a cow pasture and was quickly surrounded by the Home Guard. Recognising the severity of his injuries, they rushed him to the nearby Queen Victoria Hospital in East Grinstead, a renowned centre for burns. His face and hands were in agony, and his lungs badly damaged. Every breath was a rasping torment, and even lying in bed was painful. His charred arms were encased in saline Bunyan bags to hydrate the burnt flesh and every day he was manhandled, gently but agonisingly, into saltwater baths to clean and prepare his burns for grafts. The ebullient surgeon in charge said things would get worse before they got better, but promised he would live and heal. 'You just need to get used to the idea that things will never be quite the same.'

In the burns ward there was laughter and banter, but the faces of the patients were shocking and told Taddy quite how injured he really was. Charred, peeled, hairless, nose-less and even lipless, some were blind, and others spoke with rattling vocal cords through exposed teeth.

Taddy realised life wasn't over just because he was burnt, but he did see the horror in Betty's eyes when she first saw him. She put on a brave face, and was cheerful and encouraging, but in his heart, he knew it was asking too much for this beautiful woman to bind herself to the creature he'd become. He mumbled something about releasing her, but she became furious. 'How can you think so little of me that I should love just your face? That is a far uglier thing than any damage the fire might have done! You release me? Well, Tadeusz Lubelski, I don't bloody release you!'

In that moment, he couldn't have loved her more.

'I'm going now,' she added, 'before I say something I'll regret. Mark my words, though, I'll be back, and then we can start building our life together. Is that understood?'

He nodded meekly. She kissed his bandaged face, then ran from the ward. Outside, there was an October storm raging, slamming doors and raising ragged cheers from the restless patients. Taddy was encouraged by her response, but his mood soon darkened as his pain worsened. She would always be the beautiful woman tied to the gargoyle husband, who'd once been a fighter pilot. He couldn't condemn Betty to that life. He had become a millstone around her neck, and she was just too loyal to see it. He was no good for her.

Terribly burnt and out of his mind with pain, he'd despaired that his engagement to Betty would be a grim life sentence for her. He confessed to me that the moment he saw the ward sister pushing her trolley of controlled drugs, he decided to act. She was offering pain medication, liquid morphia, an evening dose to help the patients sleep. When she left it unattended, he grabbed a bottle and guzzled the contents. He felt himself falling but before hitting the bottom, his eyes opened with stark realisation. By destroying himself, he was breaking God's holy commandment, a mortal sin that would see him damned forever.

That act of self-destruction has haunted him ever since. Taking his life in a clumsy bid to free Betty had offended his God and cherished faith. That is why Taddy believes his soul is doomed to this purgatory, sentenced to roam Brookwood for evermore. And the irony is, Betty never did release him, nor indeed herself. She never married, nor had any children. For forty-four years, she faithfully came to see her Taddy every few weeks, still proudly wearing his *gapa* wings over her heart and shedding tears over his gravestone.

POR
T. W. LUBELSKI
302 SQDN
25TH OCTOBER 1940 AGE 24
POLISH FORCES

For Taddy the long years have been a torment. The woman he loved withered before his eyes. She faithfully tended his grave until one day — her sixty-sixth birthday, as it turned out — she stopped coming. His Betty had died, her heart still broken, and Taddy's guilt was now replaced by utter anguish.

All of which is a long way of saying that Taddy is a sensitive soul. If he sees someone getting upset, he doesn't like it one bit. I guess it all reminds him too much of Betty, God rest her soul.

'I'm sorry to hear about Tilly,' I tell him, 'but listen, I've got some real news for a change. Something pretty amazing.' I tell him what's happened. 'Luke really can smell me. He looked straight at me. That boy sees me, and if he can, maybe we can talk to him too. Can you imagine what that would mean? For the first time we could converse with the living. Our world would open up, and maybe we could even resolve some of the things that are keeping us here.'

CHAPTER THREE

A few weeks later, early on a wet and cold spring morning, a ginger vixen is hunting for her cubs. They're sleeping safely, tucked away in a den beneath the tool sheds. She freezes at an awful screeching sound, moist eyes searching nervously between the rows of cold stones. She ain't sure what she's heard, but don't like it one bit.

I'm watching her winding progress through the deserted cemetery but know all too well what it is. You see, not everything at Brookwood is tranquillity, peace and dignified commemoration. There are dark things here, born out of the savage emotions and clawing grief hanging like Spanish moss in the trees of my native Tennessee.

You see, 'The Shrieker' dates from my time. I never knew her in life, but she's been here almost as long as me. I recollect she was one of the countless widows after the Great War. They'd come, all huddled together in great long coats and wide hats, the vessels of the boundless grief and melancholy that followed 'the war to end all wars.'

The widows came faithfully year after year, their numbers dwindling as time passed. They were always so hushed and dignified, and oh so 'terribly British.'

All that is, excepting one. She was young, pale, and really quite beautiful, but with wild staring eyes and a mane of dark hair left loose in a way that was unusual for the time. She would pace like a maniac, tearing at her clothes and hair, sobbing and screaming, and frightening all of the others. They treated her like a pariah that was lost in the madness of grief, threatening to engulf them all if they didn't keep a lid on it. For the fear of that, she was shunned, as they closed their ears and hearts to her torment, echoing across what was at that time the sparse acres of Brookwood Cemetery.

Her man was an American aviator with the Royal Flying Corps. I'm told she was a Romany gypsy who fell for the charms of the dashing pilot who promised so much after the war. He was decapitated when his biplane flew into a telegraph cable, and is buried here, but didn't tarry, unlike his heartbroken lover.

One morning, long ago, her cries stopped. She was found by cemetery staff hanged from one of the Redwood pines behind the American plot. She'd been there for days, but no one had noticed the silence, nor indeed her disappearance. Unmissed by the world, she went through a profound transformation. Ever since, she's been a fleeting presence in the branches of the trees, a dark shadow moving in the corner of the eye, unnoticed until she shrieks. It is a primaeval cry of despair, like that of some great bird, carried on the wind, mournful and haunting.

The melancholy sound gets me to pondering about the men that are buried beside me. With Memorial Day coming up, I find myself sitting on my anonymous cross, wondering how it is I'm the only one that remains.

Except for the 'unknown soldiers' like me, every cross in the American plot is carved from blue-white marble with a name and home state, the sole piece of individuality permitted to us in death. I've read these names so many times and have often been struck by how these boys came to be Americans. The European origins of many seems clear from their names: Gaston, Vanmeter, Bjerregaard, Lucero, Kowalewski, Carta, Cunningham, Dupree, Wilcox and Christiansen, all of which sleep just yards away from me. And yet here we are, all Americans together, so very far from home.

Skittering between the crosses, a couple of grey squirrels chase one another. A local feller once told me those critters are American imports too, and they've taken over from the local species. I can certainly tell you the population is booming here amongst Brookwood's sequoias and American pines. This one fat feller is sitting there chewing on a daffodil bulb, one of many so carefully planted by Thomas and Luke, when I recognise an odour and know old Marshall is sidling up to me.

'Sergeant! I say, Sergeant, a word, if you please,' he says. Most folk here call me Mouse, but to Marshall, rank is real important. He's the most senior officer amongst Brookwood's dead Americans. 'I've been meaning to ask, Sergeant. Don't you think it's about time our contingent benefited from some drill practice? It seems to me our *esprit de corps* is somewhat lacking. We owe it to ourselves and our British hosts to maintain appearances and uphold the honour of the flag.'

'Well, sir, I dunno about that,' I say. 'Many of us old-timers haven't been soldiers for an awful long time. Hell, I never did get taught much drill myself. My war was pretty much all mules with not a lot of marching.' He didn't like that answer one bit, so I try a different tack. 'I know you got some regular US Navy sailors here, sir, and you'd know more about that than me, but most of the other fellers are merchant navy and coast guard, so they never got much drill either. Anyhow, most have the view they've already sacrificed more than enough.'

'They're still military personnel, Sergeant. Once a soldier, always a soldier,' says Marshall. 'It is my duty as an officer and a gentlemen to lead. There's nothing like a parade to build a ship's morale and develop the men's *esprit de corps.*'

'Well, that's exactly it, sir. Those men don't have no *corps* no more. Maybe that's why half of them are still here, mourning bodies lost and lives destroyed. Some of those Navy boys got so smashed up on the rocks, they couldn't even be identified. You really can't expect them to be enthusiastic about a parade. Not after all this time.'

'So, how do you explain that Canadian officer drilling infantrymen up and down the main avenue? There, you can hear him now.'

I look up and strain to hear what he's referring to. A voice with a Canadian accent suddenly bellows, 'Officers, take post!' Then, equally loudly, 'Guides, steady.' The sound of marching boots echoes up the tarmacadam avenue. 'Guards will march past in slow and quick time. Slow march!'

Johnny Gall of the Grenadier Guards served in North Africa and Italy and had only just completed a course at Camberley Staff College, when a V1 flying bomb fell onto the Guards Chapel at Wellington Barracks in London during Sunday worship. It was on the anniversary of the battle of Waterloo, a very important date in the history of the Brigade of Guards. It was also an opportunity to give thanks for the steady progress of the D-Day landings, which had happened twelve days earlier. The doodlebug claimed a hundred and twenty-one lives and has the dubious honour of being the single deadliest V1 attack of the second World War. The Brigade of Guards lost the Commanding Officers of the Grenadiers, Scots Guards and the Brigade of Guards' Director of Music. Gall's gravestone commemorates that tragic morning.

CAPTAIN
J. D. GALL
CANADIAN GRENADIER GUARDS
18TH JUNE 1944 AGE 25
KILLED BY ENEMY ACTION
GUARDS CHAPEL LONDON
ELDER SON OF D. M. & M. GALL
HUSBAND OF MARION
(54.G.2)

'Aw, that's just Captain Gall trying to make the newer guardsmen feel at home. Sir, you know the British are still fighting in Iraq and Afghanistan, and casualties keep coming in. We've had a dozen over the last few years and a new youngster quite recently.' Marshall was frowning at me. 'Look, Captain Gall was on the Brigade of Guards training staff. He's just doing what the Guards do best: drill. It gives the new boys some sense of security, doing something familiar with like-minded comrades. He's working with WO2 Turton, a Grenadier also killed at the Guard's Chapel and Regimental Sergeant Major McCloud of the Scots Guards, who died from an infection in 1918, despite surviving Ypres, Cambrai and the Somme. They're drilling the new boys to bring them some comfort, not to promote discipline.'

Marshall's sallow but chubby face takes on a peeved expression. 'Sergeant, you know perfectly well that Memorial Day is just a few weeks away. We owe it to our visitors to put on a good show. I've heard the American ambassador, and the commanding admiral of the US 6th Fleet will be in attendance, plus the US Naval Forces Europe band.' He's getting worked up. 'We cannot allow ourselves to be shown up by the Army. Navy Blue and Gold all the way! The U.S. Navy knows best and is never wrong.'

Anniversaries are a big deal at Brookwood. Commemorations during April 2019 would be bigger than most, because it is the seventy-fifth anniversary of probably the biggest cock-up in American military history. Exercise Tiger was designed as a series of dress rehearsals for mankind's greatest amphibious invasion: the storming of the beaches in Normandy in June 1944. The exercises were held at Slapton Sands in Devon, chosen because it was so like Utah, the main US landing beach. The disaster that occurred there was kept secret for over thirty years and is the reason why convoys of dead American boys were transported across the country in the middle of the night, for secret burial and reburial, leaving a bitter legacy amongst those who suffered and were sworn to absolute secrecy.

The disaster was a game of two halves: one was eventually acknowledged by the military authorities, but the other remains shrouded in mystery. On the night of 27th April 1944, nine vessels of Convoy T-4, including the command vessel USS Bayfield and several LSTs (Landing Ship, Tank) were loaded with men, vehicles, fuel and ammunition. Sailing from Lyme Bay, the plan was to simulate the D-Day landings at daybreak. However, during the night enemy torpedo boats hunting off the coast of Devon picked up unusual radio traffic. The slow-moving convoy was attacked just after midnight, with the *Schnellboots* swiftly sinking two LSTs and damaging a third, which limped to port. Most victims were drowned or succumbed to hypothermia, clinging on desperately for rescue in the frigid waters of the Channel.

The death toll exceeded the total casualties suffered on Utah beach on D-Day itself and is the worst single-event loss of American military personnel since Pearl Harbour. That, however, is only half the story: on the morning of 28th April

1944, the dazed survivors of the night attack were landed as planned on Slapton Sands. Reports immediately started coming in that troops were under 'friendly fire' from 'defending forces' on the beaches. Reportedly, Royal Navy guns scheduled to fire before the troops landed, to add 'realism' to the exercise, actually fired as the second wave landed.

The official death toll for Exercise Tiger is 749, but the actual figure has never been acknowledged. There are persistent allegations suggesting that a proportion of the numbers lost were added to 'D-Day numbers' to disguise the magnitude. Equipment, vehicles and human remains have since been found in the Dorset surf, rather than out in the Channel where they might more reasonably be expected to be. Dazed survivors were sworn to secrecy, but locals still talk of hundreds of coffins arriving from across the country, then disappearing into the night.

At Brookwood, we know what happened, because the coffins came here. First by the dozen, then in their hundreds. At the end of the war, they were shipped off again, some home to the States, and others to the American cemetery in Cambridge, but near enough all were here first. Many still remain, their bodies long gone, but not their spirits. Among them is the senior American naval officer at Brookwood, Commander Marshall P Haskill III, Deputy Commander of Convoy T-4, who perished aboard LST 531 and has blamed himself for the disaster ever since.

Marshall was fifth-generation Navy and always destined to be a big noise. The Maryland Haskills helped to build the US Navy, and to say expectations were high for this last son of a family of admirals would be an understatement.

His 'plebe' year at the US Naval Academy at Annapolis was in the autumn of 1935. He'd had little trouble securing a place, since the Superintendent Admiral was a family friend, and his Uncle Jack was a congressman for the great state of Maryland. He'd practically grown up on 'the yard' under the stern gaze of Tecumseh, a Native American warrior whose statue stood on the academy's lawns.

That didn't mean he had it easy. He got thoroughly 'hazed' like any other Fourth-Class Midshipman, but he did manage to pass from 'plebe' to 'youngster', and then to Second-Class Midshipman. With war clouds gathering in Europe, Marshall was a 'Firstie' with fine scores in gunnery and a reputation as a parade ground commander.

Marshall had the pick of assignments and chose to work on destroyers protecting the Atlantic convoys. He was a lieutenant when Pearl Harbour was attacked, on shore assignment at the time, helping his alma mater ramp up the output of midshipmen for the increased demand of war. Marshall then served during the North African landings, followed by a posting to England as a new lieutenant commander, working on plans for the invasion of Europe.

In late 1943, a series of exercises were scheduled at Slapton Sands in Devon, England. It had a flat gravel beach, with grasslands which led to a tidal lake, identical to Utah beach in France. Practice landings began in December, culminating in full-scale exercises on the calmer seas of April 1944. The overnight operation would involve eight tank landing ships (LSTs) and thirty thousand troops, including infantry, armour, engineers, artillery and medics.

Marshall was one of a dozen top-level BIGOT (British Invasion of German Occupied Territory) cleared officers with a full knowledge of the maps and plans for the forthcoming D-Day assaults. He was Deputy Commander of the convoy, assigned to LST 531, under the orders of Commander Skahill on LST 515 and Rear Admiral Moon on USS Bayfield.

There had been a few problems during the previous day's exercise and Admiral Moon was determined that this second landing should run smoothly. The convoy would spend the night at sea and then hit the beaches at dawn. That evening, Marshall dined with the ship's officers and those of the 1st Engineer Special Brigade. After dinner, he assembled the BIGOT level officers for an impromptu briefing.

'Gentlemen, forgive the poor jest if I say that under no circumstances are any documents or high priority personnel, that's you "bigoted" officers, can be allowed to fall into enemy hands.' His audience were polite enough to chuckle, but they'd heard the joke many times before. 'Each of you has been entrusted with most secret plans, and I cannot stress strongly enough the personal consequences to any officer who is responsible for a security breach.' His warning didn't make him particularly popular with the engineers, but he felt it was important they realised that what they knew of Omaha, Utah and Pointe du Hoc was worth more than their lives.

At one o'clock in the morning, there were the first signs of trouble. A signal from LST 507 reported hearing scraping noises beneath her hull. It would later be realised that this was the first German torpedo passing beneath the shallow draft of the amphibious vessel, a very lucky escape. After two o'clock, that luck ran out and LST 507 was struck amidships.

The attack was accompanied by shadows that darted about like dark wraiths, followed by a mass of blinding red flares, the attack signal of German *Schnellboots*. Marshall rushed to the bridge to find Lieutenant James Swartz, the vessel's captain. The Executive Officer (XO) advised that tracers had been spotted on the radar earlier, but it had been assumed they were part of the convoy's escort.

LST 507 was hit on the starboard side with soaring flames swiftly roaring through her auxiliary engine room. Onboard were a crew of a hundred and sixty-five seamen bolstered by a further three hundred Army personnel. The ship's deck and hold were crammed with fuelled-up trucks and jeeps, plus full oil barrels and wheeled bowsers. The inferno raged, with burning fuel soon pouring over the ship's sides to cover the surface of the sea. As the slick spread, the ship was struck again and began to sink by her stern. The order 'Abandon ship' was called and terrified survivors began leaping through the flames into the freezing water. Some were killed by the fire, but many more would drown. LST 289 was then struck near her crew living quarters, catching fire, but she still managed to limp away.

In the flickering light of the flames reflecting off the water, Marshall glimpsed the bubbling hiss of anther torpedo, just before it struck. This first detonation was followed by a second, and LST 531 began keeling over and would sink with all hands in under six minutes. Marshall just had time to slide down the curving side of the ship, hitting the freezing water, having lost sight of both Lieutenant Swartz and the XO.

Immediately dragged down into the darkness, his lungs screamed for oxygen as he pulled against the suction of the sea. He lost his shoes, cap and leather satchel, straining towards the brightness of the flames on the surface. Marshall was a strong swimmer and somehow managed to make his way beyond the burning fuel. There he found a cluster of flailing men, trying to stay afloat. Terrified of the encroaching fire, Marshall ordered them to swim away, but many were too shocked, exhausted or injured to react. Once at a safer distance, he watched LST

531's death throes, realising with horror that over five hundred souls had been on board.

Amongst the survivors thrashing in the sea, he spotted that many troopers were wearing their life preservers incorrectly. They hadn't been issued with USN kapok life jackets, but instead had on rubber inner tubes. Many also had their backpacks on, the flotation ring tucked underneath around their waists. Once in the grip of the icy water, shock made many panic and the weight of their packs began pulling their heads under the water. Countless soldiers drowned up-ended, legs flailing then growing still. Most were from the 1st Special Engineer Brigade, Marshall's dinner companions, but there were also men of the 557th and 3206th Quartermaster Service Companies.

As the cold and shock took hold, the cluster of men he was with dwindled. A Boatswain's Mate and a Chief Petty Officer, both veterans that Marshall knew well, were both overcome and slipped away silently, sinking into the depths. One of two lifeboats that managed to launch from LST 531 approached the group, and strong hands reached to pull Marshall aboard. The open boat was already filled with sodden, shuddering, blue-faced men, their eyes rolling into their heads.

Marshall fared little better. Neither rank nor naval experience could protect him from his fate. He died of hypothermia in the six inches of freezing water lapping across the wooden slats of the clinker hull.

Marshall is a permanently agitated man. He is always twitching and anxiously searching for his lost satchel containing the top-secret maps of the D-Day landings, and he worries constantly over the fate of the other BIGOT officers.

As the bodies began arriving from Devon and time passed, he refused to calm down, always finding something new to worry about. Worrying is probably what Marshall does best. He is on the chubby side, the legacy of a lifetime spent on ships with little space for exercise and a generous officers' wardroom, but he is always immaculately dressed in US Navy whites with gold braid and stars and a peaked white cap. None of this fine attire would have done him any good in the frigid English Channel, but I guess that's how he feels when at his best. He is meticulous, pedantic, and very conscious of rank and hierarchy, and frankly he drives me nuts. Technically, he is the highest ranking US officer at Brookwood, and therefore I guess my boss. It worried me when he first arrived, but it turned out Marshall is far too absorbed in dealing with his many inner demons to start causing problems for others.

Apart from his lost satchel and brother 'bigots,' he is constantly churning over worst-case scenarios: Were the others captured? Did their secret documents wash ashore onto occupied French soil? Should he have reacted to the radar signals? Could he have done more? Should he have done more? Was the disaster his fault? And if not his, then whose? Who was to blame for Exercise Tiger?

He agonises, eternally wracked with guilt, and when not obsessing about that, he mourns for the glittering naval career he should have had. His worst fear is that the long and noble ancestral line of Haskill Admirals might forever be linked to the disaster at Slapton Sands.

Every day he patrols the rows of what were at first wooden crosses, later replaced by marble ones. He counts, marking off names of those he's found, but endlessly worrying about the missing. In this obsessive search, he is joined by harassed 1st Lieutenant Edward Delamater of New York, the CO of the first platoon, 607th Quartermaster Graves Registration Company, who was lost with fifteen of his men when LST 531 went down. With the bitterest of irony, this former undertaker now toils under Marshall, forever trying to account for those lost and missing.

After the war, the remains of both of these officers, along with every other World War Two American casualty, were moved. Their spirits remain here, though, their task incomplete and now made more difficult without actual graves, as they frantically go through their lists time and time again. Their combined aura is of brine, seaweed and petroleum gloop. Curiously, it is also somehow mixed with the powerful stink of perpetual anxiety.

Sometime after the dead from Exercise Tiger arrived at Brookwood, news trickled through that Rear Admiral Don Moon, the Naval commander of the operation had also died. He'd gone on to command the Utah landings, but tragically took his own life on 5th August 1944. At the time, he was facing a court martial for the events that occurred in Devon, a catastrophic prospect for a career Navy man and graduate of the US Naval Academy. One wonders what was troubling his mind before the end.

Did the news relieve Marshall's guilty conscience, or did it make things worse? I've often tried to talk to him about it, but he's unwilling to consider any criticism of the 'chain of command'. He's much more concerned about the reputation of the Naval Academy and the US Navy, rather than thinking about those poor boys that still lie beneath the waves. When his grave was still here, I recall it wasn't too far from mine. I reckon he's probably back at Annapolis now, but the engraving on his headstone won't have changed:

MARSHALL P HASKILL III
LT CDR USS LST 531 USN
MARYLAND APR 28 1944

Every once in a while, Marshall tries to hold a parade, so he can count up his troops. The count never changes, but it seems important to him, and I guess it makes him feel in control. I look at him, feeling about as weary as can be. I've got no time or patience for this. 'They cannot see us, sir. It doesn't make a blind bit of difference what we do. I'm very sorry, but I cannot help you with your parade. You'll have to excuse me; I have other matters to attend to.'

Taddy comes to my rescue and ushers me away. 'Tilly is back and she's in a terrible state,' he says. 'Her eyes are all raw, and her hair is everywhere. She is so skinny. She's been lurking around the maintenance sheds — you know, where they keep the blank headstones. What can she possibly be looking for?'

'Maybe she's looking for squirrels or the foxes hiding under the sheds? There are plenty of them around.'

'Why would wildlife make her cry? I think maybe someone is sleeping rough down there. I'm not sure, but things get moved around.'

We decide we better go and check on what Tilly is up to. Taddy's right; she's far too skinny, swamped in a long coat with a big old hood hiding her face. When her coat falls open, I see she has only a tiny black vest and skirt on, despite the biting cold. Now, I know fashion has changed since my time, but I surely wouldn't want no daughter of mine dressed like that, not in this weather. She can't be thinking straight.

She hurries past the great stone urns that stand beneath the giant sequoias, placed upon the low wall that is carved with eagles. The benches there are a congregating place and a few of the fellers wave as we pass, trying to keep up with Tilly. She cuts through the portico of the American Battle Monuments Commission offices and is heading towards the Canadian plot.

The air fills with the startling crash of gunfire. That's something about Brookwood that catches out most folk. This place of quiet commemoration, where one might perhaps expect dignified silence, is often assailed by the sound of the guns. The famous shooting ranges of the National Rifle Association at Bisley are just two miles away. Consequently, there is no peaceful slumber for the warriors laid here. The noise is still shocking to many after their own brutal demise.

The Canadian plot is the largest one in the cemetery and holds 2,400 servicemen from both wars. Behind it, there is a wooded hillock which we call 'Canuck Corner', on account of the bomber crews that congregate here. I'm told the fragrant pines and fine view from up there reminds them of home. Working amongst the shadowy trees, I can see Luke and his father Thomas trimming off lower limbs. They're watched silently by a mob of airmen, sitting along the metal fence that separates the military and civilian cemeteries. Luke spots Tilly and waves her over.

'What are you doing up here, Tilly?' he asks when she joins them.

She looks away. 'I like it here. It's peaceful.'

'You heard anything from your dad yet?' Thomas asks.

Tilly shakes her head. 'Not for months. He's completely disappeared. He does that every now and again, but never for this long.'

'I'm sure he'll turn up. He always does. Always been mad as a hatter, has old Callum. Still, he's dependable in his own nutty way. He was a good pal back in the day.'

'Maybe he was your good pal, but he's bloody useless as a father,' she snaps angrily, but then catches herself and smiles. 'Whenever I see you and Luke together, I realise just how much I've missed out on. It's all very well saying "Good old

Crazy Callum, the war hero," but it's no damned fun when he's your dad.'

'I'm sorry, Tilly. I didn't mean to speak out of turn,' says Thomas. 'I'll keep an eye out for Cal, I promise.'

I can see Thomas is pained and Tilly takes a few deep breaths, trying to control her emotions. Seeing her upset makes Luke feel uncomfortable. He waves goodbye and he wanders off to get back to work.

'It's okay, talking about Dad always winds me up. I'm sorry if I've upset Luke,' she says to Thomas.

'He'll be all right,' replies Thomas, giving her a hug.

Back amongst the pine trees, Luke starts to sing to himself. As he gets into it, he bellows out a favourite hymn of his and mine: '*I vow to thee, my country, all earthly things above…*'

What Luke doesn't realise is that ranks of airmen are getting to their feet, listening, standing silently before him, and all saluting as at the boy sings his heart out.

'*…entire and whole and perfect, the service of my love.*'

His father, Thomas hears him, shakes his head in wonder, his eyes glistening.

'He's such a darling,' says Tilly. 'You're so lucky to have each other. She gives Thomas a hug goodbye and then heads off towards Pirbright and I'm guessing her train home. I really hope she's going to be all right.

'Do you think it's her father she's searching for?' I ask Taddy.

'Could be, but why would one of the living choose to hide here amongst the dead?'

'I've heard her mention that he's an ex-soldier; maybe there's some comfort in being amongst fighting men. War can do a lot of damage to the body, but God knows it can do even worse to the mind.'

Taddy nods. 'I think we must look for this lost comrade. For him, but also for the sake of our Tilly.'

'Sure, buddy, we'll do that. But first I'm gonna check on Luke. I need to see if it was a one-off or if I can make him sense me again.'

Luke has wandered off through the metal gates that are above Canuck Corner. He's heading for the tall marble-columned tombs behind the sign that tells me this is the Zoroastrian section of the cemetery. Here in their musty shadows, the earth smells damp, the air of sap and pine needles. The dappled ground is covered in fist-sized pinecones, looking a lot like the Mills bombs we had in the trenches of the Argonne. This isn't officially part of the military cemetery, but since the World War One Indian and Turkish plots lie just beyond the hill, I can still roam around here.

As I reach the top, Luke is sitting on the marble steps of the biggest mausoleum dominating the hill. He's picked up the glass pebbles from one of the fancy graves and is flicking them at the reclining form of a statue.

I step towards him, hesitate for a moment, and then pass through him. It happens again. I can feel the warmth of a human body. He stands up sharply and looks around, confused, but he doesn't seem to see me. I try calling his name, and for a moment I think he hears me. But then he sits back down, clutching his head, rubbing his temples, and the moment passes.

I'm disappointed and decide to return to my plot, but I ain't giving up. Something important is happening here. I've got to make this connection with Luke work. It's too precious not to nurture. I will try again.

CHAPTER FOUR

A few weeks later, while I'm idly watching to see if Luke will return with Thomas, Taddy joins me, and asks whether I'm going the Czech Liberation Day ceremony later that afternoon. It's being held to commemorate the Day of Victory on 8th May, 1945, when Czech resistance agreed to a ceasefire in the Prague uprising as the Germans retreated. It was just one day later that the Soviets rolled in, plunging the shattered nation into darkness once again. It is a symbolic day for the Czechs, who were then to endure decades of Soviet oppression.

'The Czech boys really want you there,' says Taddy. 'You know how upset Petr can get every year. It would be good for you to watch over him.'

Petr was a bit of a hero during the Doodlebug summer of 1944. Like many Czech and Slovak airmen, he'd escaped the occupation of his homeland in 1939, to fight on in Poland and France. Trained as a reconnaissance pilot, he converted onto multi-engine light bombers when he arrived in England. He and his best friend, bombardier and navigator Miroslav Luděk, became night fighters, shooting down several raiders during the London Blitz.

Petr and Miroslav served in the Czechoslovak flight of No. 68 Squadron at RAF Catterick in Yorkshire, then at RAF High Ercall and finally RAF Coltishall in Norfolk. By 1944, the squadron were equipped with the 'Mossie,' the de Havilland Mosquito. British-designed, it was a twin-engine aircraft built almost completely from wood and known as the 'Timber Terror'. The squadron provided night escorts for RAF heavy bombers, carried out interdiction duties over England's sleeping cities and strike support over the Normandy landings. When the Doodlebugs began falling on England in ever increasing numbers, the squadron was called back from France and reassigned to a new speciality, that of downing V-1s, a terrifying sport the Czech pair appeared to have found a real talent for.

Petr and Miroslav had been inseparable from the earliest days when paired up as refugee pilots, fresh off the boat from conquered France. They were like brothers until the day a woman came between them, but perhaps not in the way that might be expected.

They'd been on the night fighter's trail for almost an hour. First guided by the ground plotter's radar, it was now up to Miroslav to locate the raider in the pitch-black of the night sky before he could wreak havoc amongst the bomber streams. The pair's Mosquito was positioned above the serried ranks of heavy four-engine Lancaster bombers, their huge, lumbering forms silhouetted against the moonlight that was reflecting off the surface of the sea.

As they approached the Continent, an impressively strict blackout was being observed. The Mossie slipped beneath the bombers, hoping to catch a stalking night-fighter positioning for a belly shot. With any luck, a raider might be silhouetted against the sky and intercepted before it attacked. The bomber stream was being stalked by the *Luftwaffe's Nachtjagdgeschwader 1*, led by the legendary night fighter ace known as the 'Ghost of St Truiden', but were in turn being stalked by the RAF's No. 68 Squadron.

In the de Havilland Mosquito, pilot and navigator sit side by side, the pilot on the left and slightly forward, the navigator to the right and a bit back. It is an egalitarian arrangement with interchangeable roles, perfectly suited to how Petr and

Miroslav flew and interacted. Both were qualified pilots, but Petr was older, so they'd agreed he would be skipper. They flew as a partnership, each with assigned responsibilities, but neither really in charge.

Miroslav's job was to find the enemy night fighter before it attacked the near-helpless bombers they were watching over. To help him, the Mosquito was equipped with Top Secret detection systems. The Serrate radar allowed the navigator to track the enemy using signals emitted by the enemy's complex frame of *Lichtenstein* antennae, which it was using to locate the bombers. Secondly, there was a newer, even more secret device that used the enemy's own IFF (Identification Friend or Foe) system to also track them. Then, once close enough, it was down to patience, good night vision and a bit of luck as the pilots hoped to spot the flare of an occasional engine backfire, or if the predator was lit up when a bomber's gunner fired, the tracers flashing brightly.

Petr controlled the Mosquito's twin Rolls-Royce engines, somewhat overpowerful for the aircraft's light wooden structure, but capable of delivering eye-watering speed. The Mossie wasn't an easy aircraft to fly. Petr had once compared the experience to having a thoroughbred you knew could win the race, but needed to be controlled and ridden competently and firmly, all the while knowing it was quite capable of kicking and biting you.

'Have anything?' Petr asked anxiously, as he peered through the Perspex of their domed cockpit, thinking this was like flying with his eyes closed.

'Hold on, hold on,' replied Miroslav. 'Drop down a little. We're too close to the big boys for a reading. Those fools are liable to start shooting at us anyway.' He clicked a knob on the panel and peered intently into the shielded screen before him.

Petr glanced across at his friend's familiar features, outlined by the glow of the scope. There was no face he knew better.

'We should be … just below…' whispered Miroslav. 'Why can't we bloody see him?'

The darkness was punctured by a pulsing light, above and starboard of them. In the resulting glow, a prehistoric-looking creature loomed, its nose covered with grotesque antennae. Higher still, a series of bright explosions ripped open the belly of a Lancaster, illuminating the night sky enough for the pilots to make out the lettering KMR. This was the devastating impact of *Schräge Musik* guns, a newly developed upward-firing automated 20mm cannon installed in the body of the night interceptor, in this case a pterodactyl-like Messerschmitt Bf 110.

Spouting bright flames, the stricken Lancaster dropped immediately, and Petr wondered how many of the seven-man crew had survived the initial attack and were now battling the G-force trying to get out. In this darkness, there was no way of seeing any parachutes. How many of them would become *Kriegies* in the nearest *Stalag Luft* or would simply die out there in the freezing cold?

Miroslav lifted the aircraft's nose, positioning the illuminated dot of his electric gunsight just ahead of the fighter's gargoyle horns. He made an allowance for deflection, but they weren't very far apart when he pressed the firing button with his leather-gloved finger. A stream of 20-mm and .303 bullets roared out from the Mossie, as Petr lifted the nose to keep the sight on his rapidly closing and disintegrating target. Both aircraft were about the same size, but his prey loomed massively above them, a stream of flame now rippling from ruptured fuel tanks as it began to slowly tumble.

In the light of the burning raider, all pretence of stealth vanished, and startled gunners from various bombers opened up on freshly illuminated night fighters, including their own matt black Mosquito. Petr punched the steering column to the right, spiralling away from a grasping line of bright tracers. Both grunted at the sudden G-force, then as they levelled out they spotted another enemy night fighter attacking a visibly struggling Lancaster about half a mile away. Petr pulled back the column into a climb and lined up the Mossie's guns onto the unsuspecting and preoccupied predator. The enemy was made brutally aware of their presence when he fired, the rear gunner trying desperately to counter. He was too late.

The deadly stream of cannon fire and bullets raced ahead, then through the target, like a flailing bull whip. This second Bf 110 reared like a wounded stag, then collapsed in on itself under the weight of fire. It suddenly exploded in a huge ball of red flame and oily black smoke, the Mossie flying straight through, streaking the clear sides of the canopy with something dark, wet and liquid. A gory slug trail traced down the Perspex as a soggy fragment of a German airman slipped into the airstream.

In aerial combat, action is quickly over; a crowded sky suddenly becomes quite empty. Levelling out, the pair once again scanned the horizon, which was already beginning to lighten. They were now well behind the tail-end of the bomber stream and in the distance, one of the Lancasters, presumably the one they'd rescued, pulsed a fine light in their direction. In Morse, it spelt out the grateful letters T and U, meaning *Thank You*.

Two kills in one night was a good result and a reason for celebrations back at No. 68 Squadron's mess. It was an international mob of aircrew, with Brits, Aussies, Canadians and Czechs. Czechs made up roughly one half of the squadron, earning it the Czech motto '*Vzdy pripraven*': *always ready*. Unusually, the squadron's crest featured a barn owl in homage to their night fighting role.

By D-Day, the squadron was stationed at RAF Castle Camps in Cambridgeshire and were briefed on missions over Normandy with great expectations. It turned out that the reality on the ground was rather dull, with the squadron seeing little action. Offsetting this disappointment, their new accommodation proved spectacularly luxurious when compared to the digs on the Norfolk plains. As the officers' mess, they had the wing of a magnificent country house called Waltons Park, owned by the Luddington family. It had been emptied of all family heirlooms except an enormous stag's head that was mounted high on the wall of the Great Hall, the principal playground for bachelor officers.

This was the start of the Doodlebug summer, and with it came a new and challenging operational role for No. 68 Squadron's Mossies. With night-time enemy bomber activity dwindling, the squadron were retrained to intercept the increasing number of V-1 pulse-jet pilotless aircraft being launched at Great Britain. In official RAF parlance, these duties were termed 'Anti-diver patrols'. The prescribed approach was to attack the rockets at high speed and from above. The V-1s generally flew relatively low, about four hundred feet from the ground. Guided by a gyrocompass, they travelled at eye-watering speeds of up to 400 mph, which was the upper limit for Mosquitoes. Daytime patrols were set at six thousand feet, with orders to dive hard at the targets, to build up sufficient speed to catch the V-1s on the straight and level. Night-time interception required a different approach, with a greater dependence on flight instrumentation.

At night, the flying bombs left a visible streak of flame across the sky, so spotting them wasn't too difficult. The challenge was getting close enough to engage. With a warhead carrying some two thousand pounds of Amatol-39, a mixture of TNT and ammonium nitrate, on detonation they had a blast radius of six hundred yards. Travelling at speed, when attacked then detonating, this speed went from 400 mph to nought in a single devastating instant. Any pursuing Mosquito risked flying straight through the blast with potentially disastrous results.

The Czech pair soon became experts at these interceptions, downing several. Their preferred daytime approach was to fly alongside at blistering speed, wingtip to wingtip, and then try to flip the doodlebug over with their wing. This was not an endeavour for the timid, and they were doodlebug aces by the time they were sent to intercept one streaking over Kent. It should have been a textbook attack in broad daylight. They were vectored onto the target by ground control and found it quite easily. Sinister, with a dartlike silhouette and smoky exhaust trail, it was visible against a background of ripening wheat crop in the fields below. Petr fired a long burst at the soulless 'robot bomb', but to no discernible effect.

'Get beside it and flip it,' said Miroslav.

'It's flying too fast,' replied Petr. 'We'll need to use guns.' He dipped their Mosquito beneath it, losing some speed and parting the cereal crop in its wake. Pulling sharply upwards on the column, Petr attempted a belly shot, but again nothing happened.

Petr sought height again, as the V-1 pulled away, continuing its relentless journey towards London. Once above it again, he tilted the aircraft to get a better look at it streaking away.

'Don't lose it, Petr.'

Throttling fuel into the roaring Rolls-Royce engines, Petr lifted the nose to gain altitude. Once well above the target again, he flipped over, firing as the illuminated dot of the gunsight came to bear. He couldn't have loosed off more than a few dozen rounds before the V-1 spectacularly exploded.

The inverted Mosquito was lifted skywards as the powerful blast swept over them, scorching the night fighter's matt black paintwork. The blast came through the ventilation slits on the sides of the cockpit, charring the sleeves of their flight suits. Petr heaved against the tumbling force, desperately trying to get away. After a heart-stopping moment, they burst through into bright blue sky, exchanging anxious glances, both realising that was really too close for comfort.

The Mosquito began to rattle as hungry flames flickered from its portside engine. 'Shit, we've got something stuck in there. I'm going to go for some height.' Petr strained at the control column, but the aircraft was unresponsive. 'I can't hold her, Miroslav. Get ready to bale out.'

'We're too low!' barked Miroslav as Petr strained, desperately trying to clear a tall row of poplars running along the edge of a Kentish hop field. The stricken Mosquito smacked into the trees at an alarming speed, scattering silvery-green leaves that moments earlier had been gently rocking in the summer breeze. The brittle trunks snapped savagely, shearing off the aircraft's timber wings and dumping flaming fuel from its ruptured tanks. The fuselage, holding both men, crashed through the smashed trees, hitting the ground hard, then ploughed through several rows of wired hops plants in the field beyond. Both are buried in Brookwood, but not side by side and in fact sixty years apart:

PETR FRANTIŠEK
NPOR. LET.
FLYING OFFICER
ROYAL AIR FORCE
11.08.1919 — 28.09.1944

Petr's funeral was a well-attended affair. The guard of honour was led by No. 68 Squadron's 'Ace of Aces,' the Czech 'B' Flight commander, Squadron Leader Miroslav Mansfeld and his navigator Flight Lieutenant Slavomil Janáček. The Inspector of the Czechoslovak Air Force, Air Commodore Karel Janoušek, supported Petr's wife, June Sylvia Františka, flanked by a heavily bandaged Miroslav, his face scratched and bruised, a plastered arm in an elaborate rig.

It was a strange for Petr to observe. His petite, frail wife supported by his best friend. She had so often dismissed him as a lovable rogue who drank too much, but now he was her rock. It was confusing, but Petr was grateful to see them together.

In the weeks and months that followed, Miroslav seemed to have become more serious, and Petr noticed his uniform bore a decoration and he'd been promoted. By war's end, Miroslav was a Squadron Leader and Petr assumed 'flying a desk', explained why his fun-loving friend always looked so grim-faced.

One spring afternoon, the pair visited again and seemed happy and all smiles. June was wearing a cream skirt suit from a pattern they'd bought together from her favourite designer, Hardy Amies. She placed a bouquet of flowers on his grave, then bowed her head, as Miroslav saluted. They glanced at each other, smiled and then kissed.

Confused, Petr watched as they held onto each other, then turned and walked away from his graveside, hand in hand up the avenue of giant Redwoods towering over the Czech burial plot. He didn't know how much time had passed since his death, but it dawned on Petr they were now together. The flowers on his grave might even be her wedding bouquet.

How was this possible? How could they have forgotten him so easily?

But they never did forget him. Every important moment of their married life, June and Mirko shared with Petr. The birth of their two sons and finally a delightful little daughter with the same fine hair as her mother. Every visit was a revelation and joy for Petr, being part of the family's evolution. It was also a cold dagger to his heart. He would rage at their happiness, at his stolen life, tormented by their disloyalty and betrayal. He watched their lives unfold, their boys grow tall and strong, until in turn they came to the annual Czech Liberation Day ceremony wearing uniforms. Their daughter grew up into the spitting image of her beautiful mother on the day he'd married her and his heart was broken all over again.

Time and tide wait for no man, and whilst Petr remained unchanged, forever aged twenty-five, for June and Mirko, the years took their toll. Mirko died first, after a brief illness and was buried with military honours in the Czech annexe plot for *émigré* soldiers. Petr watched his twice-widowed wife sob for his best friend, torn by what he was feeling. For the many bleak years, he endured her lonely visits to Mirko's graveside, mourning for a man he knew wasn't him. In time, she died too, leaving Petr to his lonely vigil over their joint headstone:

MIROSLAV LUDEK D.F.C.
MAJOR GENERAL Let.
Sqd. Ldr. ROYAL AIR FORCE
3.01.1921 — 19.08.2004
JUNE SYLVIA LUDEKA née SMITH
14.02.1920 — 27.08.2008

As I make my way over to the Czech plot, I come across Guardsman David McMurray, who we call Mack. I'd been asked by Captain Gall to have word with him. The kid, who seems impossibly young, looks lost and real sad. I drop down beside him.

He opens up to me. 'I joined the Coldstream to see London and the world, and to get away from Scotland. I spent six months on ceremonial duty, then got sent to Afghanistan. I got myself blown up by an IED, and now I'm here. Dinnae ken why.'

'Well, son, we all stick around for different reasons. Sometimes it takes a little working out. Why do you think your family chose to have you buried here, instead of in Scotland?'

'I suppose my mother was trying to please me. I made such a song and dance about wanting to get away from Scotland. She knew how much I loved my time in London and, well, geography has never been her strong point, so I reckon she must have thought this was close enough.'

'Tell me about your time in the Army.'

Mack tells me it had always just been just him and his mum. He grew up in the west coast town of Kilmarnock in Scotland. He had nothing against it, but nothing ever happened there, and there was a big wide world waiting to be explored. Joining the army gave him his escape.

Junior entry basic training was at the Army Foundation College at Harrogate in Yorkshire and was harder than he expected. Not because it was physically or mentally challenging, but because of the range of other cadets he met there. The keen ones like him, those that wanted to make it, became firm friends. It was the others that bothered him most. Generally, they were slobs, big babies or nerds that had never left their bedrooms and yet were surprised that joining the Army might prove to be hard work. Mack saw more tantrums, tears and breakdowns during those twenty-one weeks than he had in his entire life. He missed his friends from home a bit and his mum a whole lot more, but even Harrogate's bleakness and appalling weather was already more interesting than Kilmarnock. It was his first time away from Scotland and everything was bright and new. It was the beginning of an adventure.

Mack passed enough key assessments to be allowed to choose the cap badge of his preferred regiment. He chose to become a Coldstream Guard. Always good at drill, the regiment's ceremonial duties based in Windsor and London particularly appealed. Once he'd made his choice and the less able cadets were out of the way, he began to really enjoy the remaining weeks of training. During these final ten weeks, he acquired the skills of the light infantrymen, the role of the Coldstream Guards: reconnaissance, handling machine guns and mortars and acquiring the battle tactics to fight on foot and in light vehicles. His chosen specialisation was in a fire support role, and he learnt to service and use mortars, Javelin anti-tank missiles and heavy machine guns.

Mack completed his infantry training at ITC Catterick and joined Her Majesty's Coldstream Regiment of Foot Guards after forty-nine weeks in the Army. That day felt like the greatest moment of his life.

He first spent some leave with his mum, then the rest visiting Army pals. One of them, a cheeky wee chap called Sandy, was also a Coldstreamer and lived in London. They spent a week exploring the capital, including the Guards Museum and Chapel at Wellington Barracks, plus a fair bit of time trawling bars and drinking expensive beer. He had more money in his pocket than he'd ever had, but by the look of the people and cars down south, there were plenty earning a hell of a lot more than him. Mack and Sandy were posted to State Ceremonial and Public Duties with Number Seven Company, Coldstream Guards in central London. Mack was thrilled and his mum was delighted when he spoke to her on the phone.

'I cannae believe my wee lad is guarding the queen at Buckingham Palace,' she said.

As for Mack, it was a dream come true. He took the spit and polish in his stride and even enjoyed the challenge of the endless drill and parades. As it turned out, he was pretty good at it, but did occasionally find the endless guard duty tedious. Standing stock-still as tourists tried their best to get a reaction out of you was particularly galling.

He soon made friends within the regiment and the numerous Geordies seemed to enjoy taking the 'wee jock' under their wing. In contrast to their fast-talking, wise-cracking high jinks, he felt rather unworldly and naïve, just a 'teuchter fae Scotland.' Everyone seemed so confident, cultured and sophisticated compared to him.

None more so than the Coldstream subalterns, like his own platoon commander, Second Lieutenant Sebastian du Whalley. At a gangly 6' 6", he was a fourth-generation Coldstreamer with half a dozen relatives in the regiment. Cool, languid and aloof, he was still approachable but in a superior sort of way. He always gave the impression of knowing what he was doing, even when it was clear that he didn't. Mack reasoned that was the key skill to being an officer.

Correctly addressed when off-duty as Mr du Whalley, he had the requisite sportscar, packed social calendar and a beautiful, long-legged 'gel' in tow. Mack and his squaddie mates felt rather ordinary in comparison.

In October 2009, the 1st Battalion were ordered to Babaji in the central Helmand province of Afghanistan, as part of Operation Herrick 11. This would be Mack's first operational deployment, with Mr du Whalley as platoon commander and Lance Sergeant Clough as his platoon sergeant. Mack was a bag of nerves, full of anticipation and exhilaration at the prospect of going to war. This was the most thrilling thing that had ever happened in his young life. Even the long flight in a RAF A330 Voyager was exciting, as it was his first time going abroad. The heat and the arid desert landscape did not dampen his enthusiasm for becoming a Guardsman; both felt deliciously alien, with the ever-present threat of danger. Mind you, the fetid latrines, greasy cooking smells and the stink of aviation fuel were all aspects of the 'Helmand experience' that he could have done without.

He was assigned to providing top cover on a Viking BvS10, an all-terrain vehicle with two articulated cabins. It was an amphibious vehicle, hardly ideal for the mountains of Afghanistan, but it could be deployed from a landing craft and was air-transportable by C130 Hercules or slung under a

Chinook. Effectively it was two metal boxes on tracks with a protective cage to deflect Rocket Propelled Grenades (RPGs). His was the platoon's command vehicle, with a crew of two in the front and space for up to eight in the rear. It provided a digital communications platform for patrols and as he was an HMG specialist, Mack was 'up top' in a gunner's turret, manning a ring-mounted 7.62 mm heavy machine gun. At over two and a half metres above the ground, he had 360° visibility, but was also exposed to sun, wind, sand and of course the attention of the enemy.

It took a few months before Mack was confident enough to know what he was about. He'd quickly developed a solid rapport with the vehicle's driver, Corporal Waugh, nicknamed Woof, and Mr du Whalley, the commander of the vehicle, who oversaw the communications technicians in the rear. The company had seen a fair bit of action in country, but so far had only suffered one fatality and a few wounded by improvised explosive devices (IEDs). So far, their Vikings had been fortunate and avoided any serious danger. The trio were working well and Mack was starting to feel more confident when some movement caught his eye, at the top of a long wall of dried mud running alongside the dusty road they were following. He couldn't tell what was behind it, but instinctively knew something or someone had just ducked down.

'Sir! Movement over the wall to our right-hand side,' said Mack. Corporal Woof immediately slowed the vehicle, awaiting further orders.

'I think we should take a different route back to the patrol base,' said Mack.

'Don't be silly, McMurray. That'll take far too long. These bloody Vikings aren't designed for tall chaps like me. I don't mind telling you, I'm sweating my balls off. It's all right for you up there in the breeze. You're laughing, while I'm down here boiling like a pudding.'

'He may have a point, sir,' said Woof. 'It does seem awfully quiet, and I don't like the look of that damp patch on the wall over there, just where we usually turn right.'

Mack panned the turret and gun in that direction, peering through the yellow wraparound sunglasses he'd bought at the American PX.

The roadside IED was cunningly buried beneath the road surface, just short of the damp patch on the wall. It exploded directly beneath the axle joining the Viking's front and back cabs. The wet mud patch had been deliberately positioned to be spotted, encouraging a vehicle to slow down or stop right on top of the twenty pounds of high explosive placed there.

Corporal Woof had a miraculous escape, protected by his tungsten-armoured cockpit. Second Lieutenant Sebastian du Whalley lost both his legs and would never again complain about being too tall. Guardsman David McMurray was killed on Burns Supper night, January 25th, 2010. He was barely eighteen.

Mack felt terrible guilt for leaving his mother behind. For the first few years he saw a lot of her. The regiment treated her well and he assumed her visits to Brookwood were all paid for by the Army or some benevolent fund. Otherwise, there was no way she could afford to come down from Scotland quite so often. Every time she did, though, she looked worse and worse.

His mum had always been fond of a drink, and it was increasingly clear she was finding solace in alcohol. When she visited, she was heavier, puffy-faced and increasingly dishevelled. It hurt him to see her like that, as he knew how much pride she'd always taken in her appearance. Now, when she visited, she was unsteady on her feet and prone to hysterics by his graveside. Mack loved his mother, but as a teenager, he was utterly mortified by how embarrassingly she was behaving. Her increasingly erratic behaviour began to affect him badly; he blamed himself for her sorrow, but also, perhaps selfishly, he wanted her to show more dignity as the mother of a 'fallen hero'. His gravestone surely deserved at least that:

2321816 GUARDSMAN
D.M. MCMURRAY
COLDSTREAM GUARDS
25TH JANUARY 2010 AGE 18
TO THE MEN WE HOLD DEAR
SLAINTE MHAITH

By 2013, she was no longer coming. Three years is a long time in an alcoholic's life, but sadly not for her dead son. At first, Mack worried, then became resigned, and finally just assumed the worst. He never did find out what happened to her. Before long, he began to feel that he deserved her absence.

Mack's tale is a sad one, but it doesn't explain to me why his spirit has lingered. His aura doesn't give me any clues; I just get a confusing, heady combination of cordite explosive and woodsmoke, as well as a very powerful cheap men's cologne. It's the kind of thing a young feller douses himself in before going out for a night on the town.

We need to get going if we're to make the Czech ceremony, and I encourage him to come along with me. The usual suspects are there, both living and dead. There are the flagbearers, the Czech and Slovak ambassadors, and the Scouts and their band, plus a bunch of old soldiers and their families.

The Czech plot at Brookwood is unusual, because half of it is inside the Military Cemetery, with an impressive memorial surrounded by wartime graves, situated between the Polish and

Belgian plots. Beyond it is the elegant Royal Air Force shelter, overlooking the much larger plots of Air Force burials of airmen of many nations. Alongside is a gate that gives access to Brookwood's huge and extensive civilian cemetery that seems to go on for miles. On the right-hand side of the gate is the second Czech plot, where former soldiers and their wives are laid to rest. Many were survivors of the war, who having served in Allied units were unable to return to their homeland, now controlled by the Soviets. They chose to stay and make lives in Britain, steadily gaining seniority in rank and eventually passing through old age. As the years go by, the old soldiers die. Once so dashing and young, they are now aged in comparison to their young comrades and brothers lost during the war.

Amongst the gathering I can see a number of Commonwealth War Graves Commission staff, including Thomas and several other ground staff. Luke doesn't seem to be there, though. Standing right at the back is Tilly, dressed in black once again. She's watching the proceedings, enthralled, seemingly more emotionally engaged than many of the ageing veterans, who lived through the hardships being described. At the gate between the two cemeteries, I can see Petr, my Czech pilot friend, standing in his usual place. I'm relieved to see that he's calm. Ominously, that's just when the Shrieker decides to let rip with a forlorn call that reverberates through the trees. I glance at young Mack who looks startled. He's heard her too. 'Hush now, don't worry about that,' I tell him. 'She can't do you no harm.'

I want to explain to Mack how time has stood still for the Czech folk killed during the war, but for their friends, comrades and spouses it has moved on. I can see, though, that he's distracted and not really listening. I follow his gaze and discover he's staring intently at Tilly. Without a word, he makes his way through the crowd and stands just a few feet away from her. It is a peculiar thing to behold. Somehow, she seems to sense something and then quite unexpectedly smiles. Maybe she can smell that God-awful cologne. However he's managed it, somehow it seems young Mack has made a fine first impression.

CHAPTER FIVE

Flashing blue lights strobe across the night sky, reflecting off billowing smoke that swirls through the dripping tree branches. There is a fire burning in the cemetery, and it brings to mind the awful barrages over the trenches of the Meuse-Argonne. The breeze carries the taint of acrid smoke and once the sirens stop, the accompanying silence is unsettling.

It's the eve of the 75th anniversary of D-Day, a big occasion for all of us at Brookwood. The commotion on the horizon has attracted the attention of several of my comrades. Taddy and Marshall have joined me, keen to see what all the fuss is about.

'There's trouble in the civilian cemetery,' says Taddy. 'On the other side of the drainage ditch, past the Cemetery Pales.'

The water-filled ditch is the southern limit of the military cemetery and we resident soldiers are unable to wander beyond it. The Pales is the name of a straight, tarmacked road that is further on, cutting across the enormous spread that is the remainder of Brookwood Cemetery. That ain't to say there aren't plenty more soldiers buried beyond, just that they tend to be way older than us. I've been told there are even some famous Victoria Cross winners buried out there. I'm not exactly sure why, but the 'river' as we call it is one of our hard boundaries. On the other, unknown side, there's a bleak open plot of mostly unmarked graves, where I believe patients from the local asylum have been buried for decades. It's not a spot I would want to go anywhere near, on account of the tortured souls that must surely be there.

The smoke is spreading across the water and there's fire in the sky. The mournful cry of the Shrieker echoes through the smoky treeline. Something over there is burning fiercely, and Marshall is getting antsy. 'We must do something. The fire cannot be allowed to spread. There is too much to lose. Too much at risk, so many records, too many files.'

Taddy and I exchange glances, knowing that the fire must be triggering for a man who died surrounded by flames.

Hours later, it is finally getting light when Thomas drives up in the buggy he uses to cart tools and equipment around. He's got three of his men with him, all grimy and smelling of smoke. As we listen to their chat, we learn about the fire. They're speculating whether it was kids who snuck into the cemetery or maybe a homeless person lighting a fire against the chill which got out of control. The blue lights were from the fire department, and Thomas's crew are complaining about how long it took for them to arrive.

The vast civilian cemetery is less well maintained than the military one, and is overgrown in many places with brambles, long grass and fallen timber, which must have caught light and spread rapidly. The gardeners, all ex-military, live onsite in tied cottages, and so were called out as a rapid reaction force. For them, it was still an instinctive thing to run towards trouble, but after the rush of adrenaline, they are now complaining about 'being too old for this shit'.

Working together, they eventually got the bushfire under control, but a large swathe of grassland was left charred, exposing broken, long-lost gravestones. Several of Brookwood's signature pines were scorched and the faded grandeur of a few Victorian mausolea were left streaked by the smoke and flames.

Thomas is letting the men whinge, mouthing off like soldiers always do. He thanks them for getting stuck in. 'Time to head home, boys, to get washed and changed. We need to be back at the Canadian pavilion for ten o'clock. There's still a lot to do,' he says in the voice of the Company Sergeant Major that I know he once was. 'This D-Day anniversary is a big one, and we need to get the place shipshape for all our visitors.'

A significant anniversary like the 75th of D-Day is important to Brookwood not because there are many men here dating from then, as relatively few died in the UK from wounds received in Normandy, but because it is a time when the living and dead come together.

These anniversaries are busy, colourful and lively, today's more than most. The air is full of martial music, bustling crowds and patriotic flag-waving. The gravesides are decorated with Stars & Stripes and Union Jacks alongside little wooden crosses and poppies, personalised with messages scribbled onto the pale wood. The German and Italian graves each have a little wooden cross too with a blue forget-me-not, the German flower of remembrance.

I'm greeted warmly by the Italians, prisoners during World War Two, and then the Free French who fought for the liberation of their country. They were sworn enemies in life, but convivial comrades now, united, I guess, by a European temperament. They often host noisy concerts, where one or the other will stand to entertain his Mediterranean cousins. Chief amongst them is my dear friend Antonio, who has a particularly fine voice.

These concerts can get raucous. The problems mostly come from our American contingent, led more often than not by Lieutenant Commander Marshall Haskell III. For some reason, he feels that singing offends the dignity of a military cemetery. It's been a long-running cause of discord and ain't likely to get resolved anytime soon.

The origins of the problems lie in the fact that both French and Italian plots are where the World War Two American burials used to be, before all the bodies were exhumed and relocated in 1948. Some 3,600 Americans were moved, but the spirits of many stayed right here, forming the bulk of an outspoken contingent. The 'Eyeties and Frogs' were then shipped in, but they ain't no pushovers, arguing that possession of the plots means they can do as they please. Suffice to say, I've heard these arguments many, many times and have no desire to be dragged into yet another round of the turf wars.

Looking for an excuse to escape, I spot Thomas and Luke enjoying the D-Day celebrations. I haven't seen Luke for quite a spell, so I haven't been able to test our connection further. Approaching, I see that his father is in deep conversation with Tilly. She seems happier today and more animated than I've seen her in a while. I guess it's no surprise to also find a besotted Mack lurking and listening intently from the shadows. He's unobserved by the living threesome and is hanging onto Tilly's every word. So focused is he, that he doesn't realise Luke is becoming aware of his presence. The boy is sniffing the air like a hound dog, no doubt getting a whiff of Mack's powerful cologne.

Tilly is excited, waving a piece of paper in her hand. I'm too far away to catch her words, but as I get closer, Luke is about to speak out about the smell. I don't like the way things are unfolding. I really don't want the boy getting confused or alarming his father. Quick as I can, I grab Mack by the arm and frogmarch him away.

'What's wrong?' asks Mack. 'What have I done? I wasnae doing anything, Sergeant. Just enjoying her company. There's no harm in that.'

'Listen, young feller, I think you ought to be very careful about getting too stuck on her. It'll only hurt you in the long run. Remember, you don't really know anything about what's going on in her life. Right now, she comes to visit regularly, but any one of these days she could get herself a new job or meet a boyfriend and just stop coming. Where would that leave you?' He frowns and nods reluctantly. 'Come on, walk with me a spell and tell me what was so fascinating about their conversation. You seemed completely enthralled.'

'I dinnae really know,' replies Mack. 'It was a bit hard to follow. It seems they know each other quite well. Tilly was calling him Uncle Thomas, and talking about her father, saying she'd received a letter from him. She's excited and pleased that he's all right but still doesn't know where he is. Thomas asked her to read him the letter and from what I could hear, it sounded sorta weird.'

'What do you mean?'

'In the letter, he was telling her to "stay pure and chaste, and a dutiful daughter." Then there was something about "dressing demurely to avoid the hungry gaze of rapacious men." I don't think normal people talk like that. Thomas didn't know what to make of it neither, saying, "Well, at least he's got in touch. Things will work out. Callum just needs time." They then talked a bit about Ireland, then Africa, mentioning a whole bunch of place names I didn't recognise. I got the impression Thomas and Callum had served together, and that's when you came and grabbed me.'

'That's interesting. Taddy reckons Tilly has been looking for someone hiding in the cemetery. We think it might be her daddy. Seems like a pretty strange thing for him to do, though.'

'Aye, Sergeant, but by the sound of it, that Callum's not quite right in the heid.'

'You don't need to call me "Sergeant", son. Our soldiering days are long done. We're friends now, so you call me Mouse. Everybody else does, even the bad men.'

'What bad men?'

'We got all kinds. Those who came to love war and enjoyed the killing. Men guilty and executed for terrible crimes against women and children. Some of them Nazis were real bad, but so were the racist boys from the US and the British Empire. They did some terrible things because they believed in a particular way of thinking, because they felt superior to others. Then there's those that became deranged, maddened by war or disease, and their dark thoughts and deeds have tipped the balance of their minds. Hell, we've got all that darkness and much more besides, all buried beneath these seemingly peaceful acres. Especially around Plot X. What you see looks beautiful, but it don't disguise what lies beneath.'

Plot X of Brookwood Military Cemetery is a hard place to find. It's not marked on any map of the grounds, nor was it ever. Serious investigation might reveal where it once was: tucked away in a hidden corner of the grounds, beside some decrepit-looking toolsheds and under a heap of compost, piled high with rotting leaves and vegetation.

This is where the US Army's bad men were buried, until they were dug up and relocated to France in 1949. There was originally space for a hundred graves, but only eighteen condemned men ever found their way here. These were servicemen executed for horrid crimes, all bar one found guilty of rape, murder or both. Of these, two were executed by firing squad and the rest were hanged by Great Britain's notorious family business of executioners, the Pierrepoints. Most of them were dealt with by Uncle Thomas, assisted by his nephew Albert, who went on to become Great Britain's most prolific hangman, responsible for executing four hundred and thirty-five men and women over his long career. These included two hundred and two Nazi war criminals, including the notorious British collaborator, Lord Haw-Haw, as well as *Hauptsturmführer* Josef Kramer, the Commandant of Auschwitz-Birkenau and Bergen-Belsen concentration camps.

The Brookwood executions were carried out at Shepton Mallet prison in Somerset, which over three wartime years was run by the US military. By the end of 1944, seven hundred and sixty-eight prisoners were incarcerated there, guarded by a prison staff of twelve officers and eighty-two enlisted men.

These dead are considered to have brought dishonour to the American military. They were buried without coffins or ceremony, simply shrouded in cotton mattress covers into unnamed graves. They were kept separate from all other military burials, as it was felt their crimes should not be allowed to sully the valorous deeds of those honourably killed in combat. After the war, the majority of these 'dishonoured dead' were collected from burial grounds across Europe and relocated to Plot E of the Oise-Aisne American Cemetery in Northern France. Here a total of ninety-six executed American military personnel lie beneath anonymous numbered plaques. Together, they are responsible for the murder of twenty-six U.S. military personnel and seventy-one civilians. Of the eighteen executed men that were originally buried at

Brookwood, there are men guilty of the murders of several British civilians, as well as their own comrades and officers.

As a Black man, what has most perplexed me about these men is that despite only ten percent of the US Army in Britain during World War Two being African American — that's about a hundred and fifty thousand men in 1944 — out of the eighteen executed for their heinous crimes, ten were black and three Hispanic. I don't know what that says about the behaviour of US servicemen in the UK, or the bias of military justice towards men of colour, but that just don't seem right.

One of the most troublesome of these men still haunting Brookwood is Private Lee A. Davis.

Lee and his old pal, Willy Harrison, a child-killer from Ohio, have been side by side for a long time. Lee took the long drop in 1943, a good two years before Willy did the same in 1945.

Lee was born in 1923, in a rough railroad town called Temple, halfway between Waco and Austin in Texas. It was a shabby collection of shacks, tents and saloons, full of rough characters, loose women and no shortage of hard-luck stories. The town's typically knee-deep mud, and its reputation for robbery and alcoholic stupor had earnt it the nickname 'Tanglefoot.'

Not a lot is known about Lee's early years, but it didn't involve much schooling. With his mother working on her back in a cathouse and his father unknown, his upbringing can be described as chaotic at best. He found some respite and sustenance through hunting in the backcountry and learnt to fend for himself from an early age. It can't have been easy growing up as a poor Black kid in a segregated Texas, but I don't suppose it was any worse than in Tennessee, so that ain't no excuse for turning bad. I've heard that it takes a long time for things to change in Texas, so I'm sure prejudice was bad, but hell, he had forty-five years of progress on me.

The bombing of Pearl Harbour on Sunday, December 7th, 1941, changed Lee's life. From being an aimless drifter with a bad temper, he was swept along by the wave of patriotism that followed. It was still a segregated army, and although two and a half million African Americans registered for the draft, only a million served, mostly in non-combat roles. That was when, however, for the very first time in his life, Lee discovered he was actually fortunate to have been born in ol' 'Tanglefoot'.

You see, his hometown of Temple wasn't too far from newly created Fort Hood, which was destined to become the home of the US Army's tank destroyer specialism, designed to challenge the pride of Nazi Germany, the Panzers. Drafted in with hundreds of other Black labourers, he was put to work building the camp's infrastructure. Through his hard work and diligence, he was finally accepted as a volunteer for the first Black armoured unit, the 761st Tank Battalion. The unit's ambition was to secure fair treatment and equal rights, once they'd earned their fighting men's stripes 'over there'.

Their first training camp was in the mud, swamps and appalling heat of Camp Claiborne in deepest Louisiana. Under the harsh regime of white training staff, they learned and thrived despite the widespread belief that the Army shouldn't be training Black men to use guns. Though the odds were stacked against them, the troopers of the 761st graduated onto M5 Stuart light tanks. It was a unique achievement in a deeply segregated South, and after two long years the unit finally received M4 Sherman medium tanks back at Ford Hood. The 761st were now better trained than just about any other U.S. tank battalion, many of whom had long since been deployed overseas.

By spring 1943, Lee was a loader and a proud part of a Sherman crew of five. He never did learn how or why, but that was when he was unexpectedly transferred to a role as a quartermaster's clerk, handling the supply of munitions for the battalion. Perhaps it was because he could count better than some, and he swiftly found himself part of an advance detachment sent overseas in the build-up before D-Day. After a stomach-churning crossing of the Atlantic, his final destination was Iron Gates Camp in the Savernake Forest of Wiltshire, England. It was a top-secret munition dump, located deep within the forest, but also close to the US Army 347th hospital station, set up in anticipation of D-Day casualties.

Lee had joined the army to see action and was thrilled to be serving with the 761st Tank Battalion, but he could now see that prospect slipping away. He grew increasingly bored of the mundane tasks he was assigned, and resentment grew within him. Endless hours spent hauling ammunition boxes only frustrated and angered him further. All he craved was to get back to some real soldiering.

Being in England was a delight, though. Everything seemed fresh and green, and the white folk were a whole lot friendlier than back in Louisiana or Texas. The girls were pretty too. He never really knew how to behave around them, cos where he came from, being forward with a white woman was one sure way to get a feller lynched. He would stand in the background, smoking one cigarette after another.

Sometimes, he would sneak off into the woods with his tanker's M1 carbine and do some hunting. The forest was green and lush compared to the backcountry in Texas and a whole lot cooler than the Louisiana swamps. Whilst there, he would shoot deer, rabbit, pheasant or even squirrel. He was a good shot, and he reckoned it was good practice for when he got to the Germans. His hunting trips made him popular with his squad, giving them the chance to cook up some barbeque, a welcome change to the usual Army slop. His buddy Ray, from Charleston, was a big boxer with a bent nose and was always hungry. He promised to set Lee up with a gal if he shared his supply of fresh meat.

One Saturday night, they were down at the local pub, in the beer garden out back. He was talking to a girl called Cheryl. She weren't too pretty and had on too much rouge, but she had nice hair and large bosoms that made her popular. Ray whispered to Lee, 'Them'll keep you busy all night long.'

She didn't talk much, but kept asking for more drinks.

By the end of the night, Lee had run out of smokes and could hardly see straight. By then it felt like them boobs were calling him, so he finally grabbed them with both hands.

'Oi!' shrieked Cheryl, dumping the drink he'd spent the last of his money on over his head. Standing there dripping, among all his friends and many strangers, he felt completely humiliated. The whole bar was laughing at him, and in his anger he shoved Cheryl to the ground and stormed off into the night, tears of indignation burning in his eyes.

The next morning, he avoided the fellers at breakfast, but heard them sniggering behind his back. At lunchtime, Big Ray sat with him. 'That bitch deserved everything she got,' he said supportively. 'But you better watch out. When you shoved her, she sat on a glass and got cut up pretty bad. The pub landlord called the MPs and they're out looking for you. I don't need to tell you what them white fellers will do if they catch up with you. Better lie low for a spell. I reckon you oughta head out to them woods and do some hunting until things blow over. I'll cover for you at rollcall.'

Lee spent two nights brooding in the woods. He enjoyed the hunting, but was feeling pretty low, sitting by the campfire on his own. He reckoned he would probably have been missed by now, but hopefully Big Ray covered for him as promised. How the hell did he get himself into this situation? This was not going to get him back into a Sherman. He was angry, not at himself, but at all those that had treated him unfairly: in Temple, Texas, the US Army and now the goddamned English girls.

He had built himself a little shelter, bagged some rabbits for supper and was fortunate with the weather. He could happily had stayed out there longer but began to worry about being AWOL. In any case, he'd run out of smokes and although he could handle most things, life without tobacco wasn't worth contemplating. He felt tetchy and irritable, thinking about how Cheryl had spurned and then embarrassed him in front of everyone. England was so full of girls and with all the men away at war, why couldn't he just find one to be nice to him? All he needed was one, just to taste that forbidden fruit that would have got him strung up back in Texas.

It was getting late, he reckoned about eight, so he packed up and headed for the base. He planned to slip in quietly, ready to face whatever music came his way in the morning. He pulled the belt of his gaberdine coat a notch tighter, slung the M1 carbine over his shoulder and followed the sunken road that led towards Savernake Hospital and Marlborough. The whispering woods were dark and there was little light coming from the town thanks to the blackout. He had good night vision and in any case, there was nothing out there in the darkness that a loaded carbine couldn't deal with.

He heard them giggling before he saw them. Two young women, walking arm in arm back from town on this balmy

September evening. One was taller and prettier, the other shorter and squat. He followed them, listening to their chatter and inhaling the flowery trace of their perfume until they reached the top of London Hill.

His heart was pounding as he caught another delicious whiff on the night air. Perhaps it wasn't perfume; maybe it was just the sweet smell of English girls. It stirred something within him, making his head rush, and he wondered if they might be nice to him. About ten yards back, he called, 'Hey there, y'all. Where you going?'

The girls turned but kept walking. He heard one say, 'Don't stop, it's a Yank.'

That made Lee kinda mad. He didn't want to hurt nobody, just talk some. They kept walking, picking up the pace. The tall, pretty one said over her shoulder, 'I'm a nurse at the hospital. We really must hurry, or we'll be late for our shift.'

The other said urgently, 'Don't speak to him, Muriel!'

Now that really started to make him angry. Before he fully realised what he was doing, he'd unslung his carbine and pointed it at the terrified girls.

'You stand still, or I'll shoot. I swear I will.'

The girls froze. He indicated with the gun that he wanted them to cut through a hedge into the field beyond. They negotiated a barbed-wire fence with some difficulty in the fading light and then a hedgerow. As he was stepping through, the short girl suddenly yelled, 'Run for it!' and bolted.

Lee's hunting instincts kicked in. He raised the carbine to his shoulder and fired twice, hitting her once in the head and again in the back. The force of the high-velocity rounds flung her onto the muddy roadside, where she crumpled like a discarded doll. Her companion was running too, so Lee fired several shots over her head. She stopped, cowering in a patch of brambles until he caught up with her.

He stood over her as she trembled under his glare. He spoke very deliberately. 'Either you do what I say, or you die.' She whimpered, utterly terrified. 'I'm going to count to ten... Now, take off your clothes.'

She was wearing a white Mackintosh raincoat, which she slipped out of and lay on the ground. He took off his Army greatcoat and lay it on the ground too. He had longed to touch, smell and feel an English woman, and now he had his chance.

During her ordeal, Muriel tried to distract Lee by talking, but he put his hand over her mouth and dragged her deeper into the bushes, scratching her naked body on bramble thorns.

Lost and disorientated, Muriel Fawden was found three and a half hours after the bloody body of a woman was discovered on the roadside by some milk tanker drivers, who at first assumed it was a road traffic accident. They'd heard terrible screams in the dark and decided to go looking for the source once they'd alerted the police. They were joined in the hunt by two passing nurses from the hospital and a young Army cadet.

When he was apprehended, Lee Davis had nothing to say and just sat in handcuffs, nervously chain-smoking. His court-martial was held in Marlborough on 6th October 1943 and lasted a single day. He admitted to being present at the scene but stated that he had only meant to fire over the girls' heads to frighten them. 'The murder,' he said, 'was an accident.'

Lee A. Davis was found guilty of murder and rape, which under US military law were both capital crimes. He went to his death, kicking and raging, and absolutely terrified.

Lee reeks of cigarettes, his aura poisoned by the thousands he smoked during his short life and the thousands more he's somehow managed to smoke since. He stinks of stale urine and shit too, for when a man is hanged, he loses control of his bodily functions, soiling himself in a final indignity before death. I don't suppose anyone bothered to clean him up before he was buried.

His abrupt demise has left him with a curiously hissing voice, but the vileness of his remarks and the leering profanity that spews forth is all him. He died an angry young man, raging over an unfulfilled life, resenting all the racism, segregation and discrimination he faced and his stolen opportunity to prove himself in combat. Most of all, though, he's just plain bitter about all the girls who rejected him.

Over the years, what has baffled me is his inability to recognise that he's done anything wrong. He can't see that because of him, a young girl was murdered and another traumatised for life. Lee is a malevolent presence round here, and I warn Mack not to interact with him.

CHAPTER SIX

The languid summer days of August are now upon us; the weather is warm and beautiful. This is not a time usually spent dwelling on dark tidings, but it does coincide with an anniversary of a very bleak event. It is the anniversary of Operation Jubilee, the fateful raid on Dieppe in northwest France. Described as an essential trial before the D-Day landings of 1944, it provided some very harsh lessons that perhaps needed to be learnt and gained some political mileage, but by every other measure it was a complete disaster. It is remembered as Canada's single bloodiest day of the Second World War and has the dubious honour of being the single worst day for the loss of Allied aircraft, surpassing even the grimmest days of the Battle of Britain. One hundred and nineteen aircraft were shot down, desperately trying to protect the landing vessels and troops that were massacred at Dieppe.

Almost five thousand Canadians took part in the assault on 19th August 1942, alongside a thousand British and American troops. Some nine hundred and sixteen Canadians and two hundred and ten British and Americans were lost on those blood-soaked shingle beaches. An estimated 1,950 Canadians were taken prisoner, with only 2,200 making it back to England afterwards. Amongst them were many desperately wounded men who subsequently died from their injuries. Forty-three of them are buried in the Canadian plot at Brookwood, lying in two long, forlorn rows of gravestones.

Few nations are more patriotic than Canada and the anniversary, even that of a military failure, is never left un-commemorated. Hundreds of maple leaf-inspired tulips, developed by Dutch growers to commemorate the 150th anniversary of Canadian Independence on 1st July 2017, have been planted by the graves and bloom every year. Their delicate white petals are marked with a distinctive maple leaf shape, but are also reminiscent of a wounded man's shirt or bloodied bandage. The flowerheads bow respectfully in the summer breeze at the foot of many Canadian headstones. No man is left uncelebrated, and every stone also has a maple leaf flag, leaving no doubt that Canada remembers.

The crowds gathering on this summer's day are a heartening sight for the boys, and the mood at Brookwood is uncharacteristically celebratory. The Canucks rarely disappoint, always putting on a good show, and apart from solemn moments when dignitaries and military representatives do their bit, most visitors are good-natured, upbeat and seem to be enjoying themselves. We don't often get that sort of energy around here, and truth be told some of the boys find it a mite unsettling. Me, I try to take it all in my stride, since anything different happening is a distraction from an otherwise unrelenting existence.

The usual suspects of the Commonwealth War Graves staff and friends of Brookwood are in attendance, plus the Scouts, the Cadets and the British Legion, as well as various marching and pipe bands. Amongst them, I can see the cemetery director talking to the American superintendent, standing beside Thomas and Luke, both wearing their smartest ground staff uniforms. A dozen or so of their colleagues and volunteers are dotted around the site.

Making their way through the crowd, both living and dead, Mack and Taddy appear, one wearing his scruffy modern desert combats, the other his immaculate RAF battle dress, forage cap and tie. They both seem agitated and anxious.

'What's up, boys?' I say.

'We can't find Tilly,' says a worried Mack.

'It's not like her to miss a big event like this,' adds Taddy.

'I warned the two of you about expecting too much of her. She could be anywhere. She's probably just getting on with her life.'

Mack shakes his head. 'No, it's not just us getting worried. I heard Thomas talking about it and asking his crew if they'd seen her. He told them to keep an eye out. I think he's worried too.'

'How long since you last saw her, Mack?' asks Taddy.

'I dunno, maybe a week, could be two. It's hard to tell.'

'Seriously, Mouse,' says Taddy. 'Perhaps we should all be looking for her. Thomas is a soldier and is not one to panic, and so if he's worried, maybe we should be too. I was thinking we should ask our Canadians to keep a lookout, especially since today is their big day. I'm on my way to Canuck Hill to speak to the bomber crews I know. I'll ask them to get the word out to their countrymen.'

'That's fine,' I said. 'I'll go check on what Thomas and Luke are saying. Mack, you come with me.'

We make our way through the crowds, some alive, some spirits. Two men stand out. They're not visitors, generally rather flabby and wearing bright summer clothes, nor are they in their smart military uniforms, like most of us. These two are undoubtedly military, but shabby and a bloodied mess. One leads the other, both grimy, stained and soaked through. Mack and I are frozen in our tracks.

'You can see them too, right, Mouse?' asks Mack tentatively.

We walk towards the dishevelled pair. Both are wearing dated British Army uniforms but with different badges and webbing. One has CANADA shoulder patches and a Tommy's helmet on his head. His eyes are bandaged, and he has a wounded arm strapped to his webbing. His companion wears a commando's woolly hat, Royal Marines patches, a corporal's stripe and a brown leather jerkin. Equally unkempt, he limps along, leading his companion as blood seeps through his khaki trouser legs. Their faces are grimy, and they smell of burnt cork and damp sweat.

'What the hell are you two playing at?'

'How you doing, Mouse?' replies the marine breezily. I recognise the accent, but not the face. 'It's me, Bill.'

'Bill! What the hell? You look terrible.'

'Oh, dinnae fash yersel about that! This lot cannae see us,' he replies, grinning. 'Me and Louis are just playing, trying to reminisce about when we first met in Dieppe.' His companion lifts the bandage to reveal blue eyes that twinkle with humour through the grime.

'*Salut, mes amis. Bonne fêtes!* Well, maybe not happy anniversary, but *bonne continuation* at least.' It's Louis Grenier, Corporal Bill Robertson's best friend, a Quebecois *Fusilier de Mont-Royal* who died by Bill's side when returning to Newhaven after the raid.

'What's all this?' I ask. 'How d'you manage to look like this?'

'There's no harm in it, Mouse,' says the Canuck. 'Just our way of remembering.'

'Yeah, but how did you manage it?'

'I dinnae rightly know, you sort of wish for it and it just happens. You should try, takes you right back.'

'No, no. I'm very happy to leave all that well behind me,' I say, horrified at the very thought of reliving what I've spent years trying to forget. Standing before me, they smell of the sea, but with cordite and the metallic iodine of either seaweed or blood. I'm really disturbed by their appearance; I've never seen them like this, presumably the state they were in when they passed. They've told me their story before, of how the choppy grey waters of the English Channel matched the pallor of the hundreds of nauseated boys lurching through the terrible swell on the long and bitter night before the raid.

The first wave hit Red Beach just before dawn, but the shoreline wasn't visible to the flotilla of ships holding the following wave, due to depart at 07:00. The sloping pebble beach was shrouded by the smokescreen laid down earlier by light bombers. Men of the Royal Hamilton Light Infantry and the Essex Scottish Regiment — Canadian regiments, despite their names — were the first to land, accompanied by Churchill tanks of the 14th Regiment, also known as the Calgary Regiment. Before the landing, a naval bombardment of the town's defences was followed up by strafing runs from five squadrons of RAF Hurri-bombers. The second wave of the *Fusiliers de Mont-Royal* were at the ready, with 'A' Troop, 40 Commando Royal Marines in reserve.

No message had been relayed back to the anxious men of the second wave, that the first had been unsuccessful. If they could have seen the obscured beaches, it would have been to observe the Hamilton and the Essex Scottish being cut to pieces by the HMG emplacements dug into the cliff escarpment and dominating the landing zones. Survivors were now cowering behind the sea wall, their armoured support struggling to even cross the *galet* pebbles, many getting stuck with clogged tracks, too late to be of much use. Out of the twenty-nine tanks launched, two sank in deep water and twelve slipped their tracks, becoming sitting ducks for the enemy's anti-tank gunners. Only fifteen made it as far as the sea wall, which then proved to be an unbreachable, blocking their entry into Dieppe itself. Fierce enemy fire prevented the accompanying engineers from clearing the entry points, leaving the tanks stranded on the shingle. One after the other, they were taken out even as retreating infantry clustered behind them for shelter from the torrent of gunfire. All would eventually be destroyed or captured. Not a single Churchill made it off the beach.

In the meantime, the second wave were preparing to go in, oblivious to the chaos awaiting them. As the Fusiliers disembarked, they were met by intense HMG and mortar fire. Potato masher hand grenades rained down from positions above the beach. Lieutenant Colonel Dollard Ménard, the Fusiliers' commanding officer, was immediately wounded and was hit a further four times before being evacuated. He would eventually survive the raid, the only regimental commanding officer at Dieppe to do so.

Sheltering near the fallen colonel was a slim twenty-four-year-old French-Canadian lad in a battle dress that was too big for him. Desperate for someone to follow, he lifted his head to look and was immediately struck in the face by mortar shrapnel that had exploded when it struck the pebbles. His name was Louis Philippe Grenier from Montréal, Québec, and he felt he'd just been punched in the eye by a heavyweight boxer. Falling face-down in the damp shingle, he felt the pebbles press against the bridge of his nose and throbbing forehead. He had the metallic taste of blood in his mouth and began to choke, so he rolled onto his back, trying to catch his breath. When he opened his eyes, he could see nothing but terrifying blackness.

When he tried to get up, rough hands forced him down. A gruff Scottish voice said, 'Stay doon, laddie. You've taken a ding to the face. Nothing to worry about, bonny lad. I'll put a wee bit of gauze over it.'

His new friend bandaged his eyes with remarkable tenderness, then gave the parched boy a drink from his canteen. Overhead, machine gun bullets whined and ricocheted, punctuated by the dull thud of a mortar round.

'Keep your heid doon. It's proper kicking off up here.'

'*Merci, merci*!' cried Louis.

'A Frenchie, are you? *Ou est le vin ordinaire?* That's about all I know,' the Scotsman chuckled. 'Right, you sit tight now and I'll be back for you.'

Corporal Bill Robertson of 40 Royal Marine Commando left the young Canadian Fusilier as comfortable as he could. *Christ*, he thought, *they've made a right mess of his face.*

Bill had watched the landing craft pull away from the motor transport that had brought them all over from Shanklin on the Isle of Wight. As soon as they'd entered the smokescreen, he knew something was wrong. He'd heard enough incoming gunfire at St Valery to recognise when someone was in big trouble.

The Marines' orders were to land by motorised gunboats onto Dieppe's docks, once captured by the first waves. Their task was to destroy the harbour installations, and recover certain key documents, known to be located at the Dieppe post office. As they headed in, there was a last-minute change in the orders, with new instructions to support the *Fusiliers de Mont-Royal* in taking the town centre. Bill didn't like the sound of that, but in the ensuing chaos he switched onto a landing craft. He put his reservations to the back of his mind, keen now to just get going. It took half an hour before they were actually underway, a useful interlude for the enemy to prepare a warm reception.

Even as the Royal Marine landing craft approached the shoreline, they were engaged, taking heavy damage and numerous casualties whilst still offshore. The craft that did make it to the beach were confronted with utter devastation, men surging forwards to the town centre and getting mowed down. This was when and where Bill found Louis, although neither knew the other's name.

As the Marines moved forward, the weight of fire worsened, and men desperately sought cover wherever they could. Bill hid behind a flaming Churchill that was wedged up against a concrete anti-tank obstacle. The AFV had been hit several times and hanging from the rear hatch was the charred torso of a crewman sizzling nauseatingly above Bill's head. He quickly checked that nothing nasty had dripped onto his woollen cap before moving away. Glancing back at the landing craft at the waterline, he could see Lieutenant Colonel Phillipps, CO of the Marine detachment, standing completely exposed and waving his arms, desperately trying to get his men to withdraw. He was caught by a burst of HMG fire and tumbled off the stern into foot-deep water, stone dead before he even got wet.

Heroic maybe, but very stupid, thought Bill, tucking himself behind the bogies and track of the burning tank, as another prolonged burst of fire rattled overhead.

'Right, I'm oot of here,' he said to himself, before slithering back down the shingle towards the waterline. On his way, he checked on the crumpled forms of stricken comrades but found no-one breathing. Increasingly frustrated, he was determined to find at least one to bring back with him, away from that accursed beach. The next inert body stirred unexpectedly, and he recognised the lad he'd bandaged earlier. It was less than an hour ago but felt like a lifetime.

'Hello there, laddie. I told you I'd be back,' he said. 'Come on, let's be having you. Time to go. Getting a bit sticky out here.'

'You came back? *Dieu merci!*' said the lad, groping blindly at the sound of Bill's voice.

'Take it easy, son,' said Bill. 'Now, you just listen to old Bill. You're going to put your hand on my shoulder and hold onto it. Whatever happens, you hold on tight. I'll tell you when to stand and when to walk and run. You got it?'

'*Oui, monsieur,*' said Louis, nodding. The gauze over his eyes was soaked through with blood. Thin rivulets were running down his face, soaking into the collar of his oversized khaki shirt. Bill could see his skin was like blue marble from blood loss, and the boy's fingers trembled as he clung desperately to his shoulder straps.

'Right, here we go. Get ready, and up we get. Now let's walk, nice and steady.'

Together they stumbled through the pebbles towards the waterline, mercifully unmolested by the enemy's fire. They were fortunate, but that luck couldn't hold. Machine gun fire from the clifftops stitched back and forth, splashing like skipping stones across the water's surface. When it reached the shoreline, bullets ricocheted off the pebbles. Bill was hit with a terrible smack to the groin. He tumbled over, pulling Louis down with him. The petrified boy called out, getting louder as he received no reply.

A few metres away, he heard Bill growl in his distinctive accent. 'Will you shut up! You're attracting their attention. Just give me a second. I feel like I've been kicked in the nuts by a mule.' He nervously unbuttoned the flies of his battledress trousers and reached in with his hand. Everything seemed intact, except for the pulsing wet hole in his inner thigh that had already soaked the front of his trousers. He felt no pain, but the numbness was worrying, not least in this most sensitive part of his anatomy.

'I'm fine, laddie,' he said, trying to calm Louis and convince himself. He took the boy's hand and placed it back on his shoulder. 'Right, let's get going. We need to get to that boat before it leaves the beach. Anyone left here is either dead or going to end up a prisoner. I don't fancy either option. *Comprendez, mon ami?*'

Chest-deep in the chilly water, Bill waved frantically to the helmsman of the nearest motor launch. He beckoned them forward. From the back of the launch two mortars were firing furiously, taking the fight back to the enemy dug-in on the cliffs. In response, the vessel was targeted by more fire, dinging noisily off its metal surfaces. Bill caught another painful ricochet, this time through his palm.

'Och, you dancing bear, that bloody hurts!' he groaned.

Alarmed, Louis asked, *'Qu'est ce qui ce passe?* Are you hit, *mon ami?*'

'Aye, I'm fine. Come on, we need to get out of here.'

Strong arms reached down from the launch, grasping their outstretched hands. With a mighty 'Two-six heave!' the two exhausted men were pulled aboard. Soon, they were settled under cover, alongside several other wounded men. The flashes on their shoulders showed the array of units that had been thrown at the beach. Under heavy fire, the boat's skipper decided to pull away. Within moments, orders over the radio instructed all small vessels to evacuate personnel from the beach, and return to the transports and escorting destroyers, before returning to England.

The Dieppe raid was over after less than six hours and was considered an unmitigated disaster. Almost eighteen hundred men had been killed, with over six hundred wounded and almost two thousand captured. The Royal Navy lost thirty-four vessels, including a destroyer, the RAF over a hundred aircraft.

The enemy's losses numbered over three hundred killed, with an anti-submarine vessel sunk and forty-eight aircraft lost.

The burbling of the launch's twin props lulled Bill and Louis to sleep, exhausted from their exertions and blood loss. They were barely conscious by the time the vessel reached the destroyer HMS *Albrighton*, which would ferry the survivors to Newhaven for debriefing and hospitalisation. Both men were strapped to stretchers before being swung aboard the larger vessel. Each was given a perfunctory examination by a harassed medic. A second bandage was wrapped around Louis's sodden gauze, and Bill's trouser leg was cut open. After some painful probing with forceps, his leg was bandaged tight, and he was given a blanket to protect him from the brisk sea breeze. No one paid much attention to the slick of blood where the pair had lain.

Once on the destroyer, they were allocated adjoining cots and given pain relief and plasma. Bill listened to the conversations around them. Most survivors were delighted to have made it through the carnage, but many were angry. A red-headed lieutenant of the Essex Scottish, his arm and shoulder in a sling, growled, 'They knew we were coming. Those guns waited for the first wave to land.'

'Calm down, Lieutenant Trudeau,' said a rotund Army captain, wearing the same grimy uniform as his subordinate. He was lying with his legs strapped together in a makeshift splint. 'We may just have attacked at the wrong time. Dawn was always going to be when the enemy stands to. Fair weather and a favourable tide probably put them on alert.'

'What?' replied the hot-tempered lieutenant. 'What you're saying, sir, is that we never stood a chance of catching them by surprise?'

A sergeant major of the *Fusilier de Mont-Royal* interrupted. 'My apologies, *mon Capitaine*, but I fear you are wrong. We captured prisoners on Red Beach, and they boasted of being brought in especially for the raid. They've been waiting for us for a week. *Le lieutenant* is correct. *Ils était certainement avertis.*'

A bare-headed tank crewman, his face smeared with black soot, added, 'When we came ashore, the artillery fire was far too accurate. We got hit almost immediately and my tank BEEFY caught fire. I baled out and hid under it until things quietened down. That's when I noticed a yellow stake hammered into the ground beneath our tracks. I spotted several more as I made my way back down the beach. The whole area had been pegged out into fire zones. I'd say they were definitely ready for us.'

Louis stirred, hearing the voice of his platoon commander, *Sous-Lieutenant* Michel Langlois.

'I was leading a section into town, and we sheltered in a fisherman's hut near the quayside. Inside, two terrified women said their husbands had been taken away *par les Allemands*. They gave us some water; it's all they had, *les pauvres*. They said *les Boches* had been preparing for weeks and all the fishermen were forced to help build the defences.'

The return to Newhaven took several hours. Louis became concerned that he hadn't heard his protector's gruff voice for a while. He reached out his hand in the direction of Bill's shallow breathing, fluttering his fingers up a bandaged leg to find a large, callused hand. He gripped it and was rewarded with a faint response from the Scotsman. Their clasped hands were sticky with blood.

Strong as he was, the big Marine was the first to die. The leg wound had damaged the femoral vein and nicked the artery. In the confusion, it was easily missed, but proved fatal for Bill.

His hand grew heavy in Louis's grip until he finally dropped it. By then, the throbbing in Louis's head had grown into the worst headache of his life. The massive brain haemorrhage in his skull was invisible, except for a thin line of blood that escaped his nostril. Louis's darkness became permanent soon after.

They are both buried on the Canadian plot at Brookwood, just a few rows apart, Louis with his comrades of Les Fusiliers Mont-Royal, Bill on his own at the end of a row.

PO/X3497 CORPORAL
W.A. ROBERTSON
NO.40 R.M. COMMANDO
19TH AUGUST 1942
HE WILL NOT AGE, HIS SONG IS SUNG
AND HE REMAINS FOREVER YOUNG

D.62923 PRIVATE
LOUIS PHILIPPE GRENIER
LES FUSILIERS MONT-ROYAL
LE 19 AOUT 1942 AGE 24
A LA DOUCE MEMOIRE
DE CE BRAVE SOLDAT
HEROS DE DIEPPE
(38.C.5)

Thinking on Bill and Louis's story makes my mind wander, when I really need to focus on finding Tilly's whereabouts.

'Listen, boys, I need your help on something. I've got a mission for you, if you will.' They stand straighter, now listening with rapt attention. You can take the men out of the service, but not the service out of the men. 'You know Tilly, that kinda sad-looking girl who often visits. Mostly dressed in black.' They both nod. 'Well, young Mack here is kinda sweet on her, and hasn't seen her for a while and is getting a mite worried.'

They snort at Mack's expense, and he starts to go red, but they're both listening. 'I wouldn't usually be concerned, but it seems her living friends are concerned too. I'm going to go see what else I can find out, but in the meantime, could you keep your eyes open and maybe spread the word?'

Louis lifts the blooded bandage off his eyes. '*Elle est gentile, la petite,*' he says. 'I often see her put a stone on Murray Bleeman of the Royal Hamiltons' grave. He's in my row. He's the Jewish kid who made it back to England, but never woke up.'

'Aye,' says Bill. 'Sure thing, we'll spread the word. Let us know if you learn anything from the "Live Bawbs". That's what I call them who are still kicking.' He gives a gappy grin.

Bill was a Royal Marine from St Andrews in Fife. There aren't many Marines at Brookwood, so he's become an honorary Canuck, accepted because of his efforts at Dieppe. I've heard him say more than once that if he'd survived the war, he would have emigrated there. There was nothing left for him in Scotland. He'd had a tough war, barely escaping St Valery when serving with the 8th Argyll & Sutherland Highlanders in 1940. He then volunteered for the Royal Marine Commando, passing their tough course at Achnacarry Castle. It was just two weeks before Dieppe that he learnt that his brother, wife and two daughters were killed in one of the few air raids on St Andrews on August 6th, 1942. He returned to France determined to exact his revenge.

I leave them to it, as Mack and I scour the crowds for Luke and his father. We find them outside the tearoom in the Canadian pavilion. It's a sandstone building, a gift from the people of Canada to the Commonwealth War Graves Commission. It's decorated with an elegant maple leaf motif and is referred to as 'Beaver House' because of the carved stone beast above the mantle. It's not a good representation; the carver had clearly never seen one. The Canucks find it hilarious, calling it the 'bald bear with a propeller'.

I can see Luke tucking into a piece of carrot cake as he follows his father distractedly. They're heading through the Canadian plot towards the Royal Hospital Burial Ground. You see, not all the past residents of the famous old soldiers' home are buried at Brookwood, but a good number are. The distinctively attired Chelsea pensioners are regular visitors to the cemetery and have been buried here since 1962. Over a thousand have been laid to rest in what is still called the 'new' Royal Hospital plot. It's actually a bit of a dead zone for us who remain as spirits, since although some of the names are familiar — those who died of old age — none have tarried. That's not to say they don't carry the same scars, traumas and memories as we do, just that they carried them in life before being liberated by their deaths.

Thomas seems to be searching for something. I can only assume it's Tilly. What she might be doing here amongst the rhododendron bushes surrounding the Royal Hospital plot beats me. I see him lifting up undergrowth and peering under branches. All the while, Luke is muttering to himself as he follows his father. I ask Mack to keep an eye on him while I go after Thomas. He's now crouched low under a particularly dense thicket and has found a spot where someone or something has lain for some time. He searches the ground methodically, and I can see where grass is crushed, a sapling has been broken, or a few leaves have been stripped off. He covers the ground expertly, searching for spoor, tracks or anything that might be unusual on the terrain. He's obviously done this before.

There's movement in the undergrowth, the sound of sighing. Thomas freezes and drops to a defensive stance, ready for any threat. He places his feet deliberately as he advances noiselessly. The air is still and warm, filled with droning insects. Away in the distance, there is the noise of the crowd and the forlorn sound of a bugler playing the 'Last Post'. In the trees, I can hear the Shrieker joining in. A moan escapes from the long grass and the word 'Yes' is gasped breathlessly.

'What the bloody hell d'you think you're doing?' roars Thomas. 'This is a cemetery. A place of respect. Get your bloody clothes on before I call the cops.'

There's a high-pitched yelp and an indignant male voice protests, 'Why are you poking about here? Are you some kind of pervert...?' He stops gabbling when he sees the burly and clearly seething Thomas. I push through the grass to find a young couple, more naked than dressed, desperately trying to cover up. The girl is slim and blushing from embarrassment. The boy is tall and pale, his bony body blotchy from the itchy grass and sunburn. They get dressed quickly, clothes inside out, buttons misaligned, underwear and shoes clutched in their hands, scuttling away as fast as they can from Thomas. Reprimanded but unrepentant, they're already looking for somewhere else to resume their amours.

Thomas takes a deep breath, hands on his hips. Something catches his eye. A short distance away, the foliage has been cut and formed into a thick mat. The crushed vegetation smells a little stale. Thomas drops to his knees, recognising what he's found. This is what the British Army call a bivvy and looks professionally constructed. It's a well-disguised observation point with good visibility in several directions.

The idea that Tilly would want to stay somewhere like this overnight seems very surprising. The mosquitoes alone would be a deterrent at this time of year. I kneel down, hoping to catch sign of her, maybe hidden in the shadows beneath the low-hanging shrubs.

'So, this is where you've been hiding?' says Thomas. 'What the hell have you done with her, Callum? God help you if you hurt that girl. I'll track you down and gut you like a fish.'

I can see his hands are trembling, and he takes a moment to compose himself before emerging from the thicket, but the man Callum isn't there. Thomas seems sure this was his hiding place, though. I decide to keep an eye out for him.

I glance at Mack. 'Come on then, let's see if the Canadians have come up with anything.'

It's always a favourite hang-out, but today Canuck Hill is heaving. I can see various shades of RAF blue, and since many are entire bomber crews, they're grouped in sevens for crashed Lancasters and fives for Wellingtons, but all are in their twenties. There are Canadian Army and Navy boys here too, plus veterans of the first war when the Canucks responded to the Empire's call the first time at such terrible cost.

Hurricane pilot Jack Benzie is amongst them, playing a skirling tune on his bagpipes. He's usually at the centre of things, perhaps subconsciously trying to get noticed. He's like me, buried under a 'Unknown RAF Pilot' headstone. His remains were found in 1976, thirty-six years after he crashed into the Thames estuary, but without sufficient evidence to provide an official identification. This anonymity really grates on old Jack, so he's always the life and soul of any Canuck party. Today, they've been joined by Commonwealth and Allied comrades, the Yanks, Poles, Czechs, Belgians, Turks and many others. Even former enemies are invited, all together now with no lasting animosity.

I ask Taddy if he's heard anything. He shakes his head. I tell him what I learned from Thomas.

From high above us in the dark canopy of the firs, a voice hisses, 'I know where she is, but y'all gawd-damned fools ain't never gonna find her.'

It's the Texan drawl and rope-crushed hiss of Lee Davis, hidden up there somewhere. I can hear the snot-thick giggle of Willy Harrison too.

'You better tell us what you know, Lee,' I call up.

'Please,' Mack says. 'Help us.'

The Canadians are unhappy that their party is being spoiled. Bill calls up, 'You, laddie, get out of the fecking tree! You're not welcome here.'

Lee disappears with a laugh. If he does know anything, he ain't ready to tell us about it yet.

CHAPTER SEVEN

The flashing blue lights are back. Strobing against the dark pines, they seem jarring and disrespectful. A police car at the cemetery is unusual, but at least no siren is sounding.

The car's driver collects a badge on a lanyard, reaches for some paperwork and climbs out. The vehicle bleeps and he hurries up the steps of Beaver House. He's tall, well-built and in his mid-forties, good-looking in a tired sort of way. He's in a crumpled suit and his badge says Detective Sergeant Andrew Moss of the Surrey Police.

What's a cop doing here? I wonder. After a little while, Juliet Barnes, the Commonwealth War Graves Commission director at Brookwood, Thomas and the policeman emerge from a side door with coffee mugs in hand. They're holding their meeting outside, on account of the warm weather. That coffee sure smells good. It's been a long, long time since I had me a good cup of Joe.

'Thank you for coming so promptly, Detective Sergeant Moss,' says the director, carefully placing her CWGC mug on the arm of a memorial bench.

'Well, thank you for telephoning Ms Barnes,' says Moss. 'After your call, I pulled up the file on your Matilda White and I found quite a long list of family disturbances on record, so I thought your "Missing Person" report merited a swift response. I know Brookwood well, so I'm keen to handle things personally. My grandfather is buried here in the Chelsea Pensioners' plot — Corporal Francis Moss of the Royal Leicestershire Regiment.'

'Nice to keep things in the family, so to speak,' says the director. 'You see, that's why we're all so desperately worried about dear Matilda. She's really part of our Brookwood family and we're terribly concerned.'

'Why would you be worried, Ms Barnes?' asks the detective, his pale eyes narrowing.

Juliet clears her throat. 'Well, perhaps it's better coming from Thomas. He knows the family so much better.'

Thomas nods. 'I've known Matilda since she was born. Her parents and I go way back. I served with her father in the Parachute Regiment. He went on to bigger things in the Army, but when I left, I kept in touch.' He looks away. 'It's fair to say that Callum White — that's her dad — was always ... well ... highly strung, but a hell of a soldier. He gave his wife, Carla, quite a hard time of it when he was off on deployment and sadly also when he was back.' Thomas coughs. 'I wouldn't say it was a great family environment, as your records no doubt confirm. By all accounts, Matilda had a tough childhood.

'Even as a little girl, Tilly liked to visit Brookwood. Then when her mother died a few years ago, she got interested in history and genealogy and started coming more regularly. She always said she found the calm and order to be "a reassuring hug". She got to know the staff here and I suppose we became a sort of surrogate family for her. My son Luke is sixteen, a similar age to her, and they are good friends. He's missing her terribly.'

Moss looks up from his notebook, an unnerving look in his eyes. 'Does your son work here too?'

'Yes, he does. Thanks to Ms Barnes, he has a place with me, sort of like my assistant, helping out with things.'

'He's a lovely boy,' says Juliet. 'It's our pleasure to have him here.'

'And how long have you worked here, Thomas?' the detective asks.

'About ten years now. Since my last tour of Afghanistan, when I left the Army. I took a horticultural management course when I got out and was lucky to get this gig. We've got quite a few ex-servicemen on staff. We like the calm and quiet.' As if on cue, Bisley's rifle ranges start banging away. Thomas snorts. 'Well, some of the time.' He waves off a buzzing fly. 'In any case, it's an honour to care for fallen comrades, and for many of us, it allows us to process some of tough things we experienced in the service.'

Moss nodded. 'It might be useful to have a chat with Luke. Would that be all right?'

'Sure, if you think it would be helpful.'

'Just to get the full picture,' says Moss. 'But tell me, Thomas, why are you so worried for Matilda?'

Thomas rubs his face. 'We've not seen her for weeks. I've tried calling her and I popped over to the flat at the weekend. No sign of her. It's not like her to just disappear like that, although the last few times I saw her, she seemed distracted and upset. She'd received a letter from her father, who's been missing for a while, and seemed anxious about that.'

Moss shrugged. 'Well, she's a young woman in her early twenties. Perfectly at liberty to go anywhere she wants. Do you know of any reason why she might be depressed or distraught? I'd hate to jump to conclusions, but do you think she may be a suicide risk?'

'No, I don't think so,' replies Thomas. 'It's just...' Moss waits, and Juliet nods her encouragement. 'Look, I'm not sure, but ... well, Callum White has a complicated military and medical record. If you have the clearance, I suggest you take a look into that. All I can say is that he's pretty messed up and has been missing from Matilda's life for a while. The last few times I saw her, I got the impression she thought her father might be hiding up here somewhere and seemed to be looking for him.'

'Sleeping rough in the cemetery? Why would he do that?'

Thomas's eyes take on an unnerving, steely quality. 'For the same reason all of us former servicemen are here. To try to find some peace. Civvy street can be a tough, disappointing place when you've served your country and then been spat out.'

'I understand. I'm sorry if my questions are upsetting,' says Moss, flicking back to a previous page of his notes. 'Have you seen any signs of an intruder on the grounds?'

'Well, we have all kinds of visitors, so it's hard to tell, but I did think that someone has been fiddling with things, moving them around. I thought it was probably just kids up to mischief, but then a few weeks ago, we had a fire. It may be unconnected, but after not seeing Matilda for a while, I was getting worried, so I went out looking in earnest. I found a well camouflaged bivvy, laid out like an OP, like we were taught in the Army.'

'OP? I'm not familiar with that term.'

'Observation Post. It's an Army term. We all know what a camouflaged OP looks like. Callum surely knows too.'

'Well, in that case, if he *is* hiding here, I'm surprised you didn't find him. If you've found his hiding place, surely it's just a question of waiting for him to return?'

'Look, I think you need to look up Callum's file,' Thomas answers flatly. 'You'll find that if he doesn't want to be found, neither you nor I, nor anyone else will find him. This is what he does, but none of that is really relevant now. What is, is that his young daughter, who has been desperate to find him, has now vanished. I don't like it. I want to find him as much as anyone, but I need to find her more.'

'And why's that?'

'She means the world to my son and…' His voice breaks with unexpected emotion. 'I promised Carla before she died that I would keep an eye on Tilly. If I've failed and she's been harmed, I'll never forgive myself.'

'I understand. Please don't get upset. How about you show me this OP and maybe I can catch Luke too?'

'Sure, that's fine. The bivvy is in a thicket of rhododendrons not far from the Chelsea Pensioners' plot, so you can visit your granddad while I go and fetch Luke.'

'Great.' The inspector turns to Juliet. 'Thank you for your time, Ms Barnes. I'll be sure to check in with you when I have progress to report.'

She offers him her hand. 'I'd be most grateful, but please liaise with Thomas. He knows her best.'

It is good to know that Tilly's disappearance is being looked into officially. For our part, we'll keep working on Lee, to see if there is any truth to his tall tales. He's enjoying taunting the others about what he knows or doesn't know. Willy, too, but in his drunken haze it's harder to tell.

It's a tedious game. Many are just tired of it, but Bill, Louis, Taddy and Mack are getting angrier and more exasperated. Nothing is forthcoming from Lee, Thomas or that policeman, and I'm pretty angsty too. They took Luke away for questioning, but he's back working in the gardens so they must have released him. I'm supposed to keep close to Thomas and Luke to see what I can learn, whilst the others are working on our belligerent pair of convicted murderers.

Thomas is digging over some weedy ground by the gravestones in Military Annexe 133. This is where the most recent burials are held, like the trooper from The Royal Lancers who joined us in February of this year. Young Mack's grave is nearby too, as is Lance Corporal Chris Thomas of the Welsh Guards who was lost in the Falklands War. We have the fallen from the troubles in Northern Ireland too, from various accidents, terrorist attacks and the seemingly endless conflicts in Iraq and Afghanistan.

The recent graves get more visitors than the rest of us, with fresh flowers, wreaths, poppy crosses and many other personal mementos. The CWGC's policy is to keep all gravestones unified in appearance, so the offerings are tolerated until they become tatty or decay, and then are subtly removed. It's a heart-breaking duty for the cemetery's gardeners to remove the drawings or cuddly toys left by a child for their lost father or a grieving mother for her son. As Brookwood's head gardener, Thomas takes on this difficult task himself. I admire him for that and notice that he allows flexibility with the rules, forgiving a handsome handmade wooden cross, the simple plaque commemorating a lost mate from No. 1 Guards Para, the painted pebble reading 'From Lucy to her daddy' and the laminated Welsh dragon with the simple words 'Remember Me.'

I'm watching him bag up the brown remains of spoilt bouquets, ruined by the recent rains. His is an obvious military bearing, the moustache typical of a British Army NCO of a certain vintage, with the mottled blue tattoo of the Parachute Regiment wings on his forearm. He's broad-shouldered, with close-cropped silvering hair and the callused hands of a practical man who can take care of himself.

From inside his waterproof green jacket, his mobile phone rings. It took me a while to understand the concept of a portable telephone, but once it was explained to me by one of the more modern fellers, I finally got it. Still makes me jump, though, whenever someone starts to ring, and I find it a mite peculiar to see people striding around talking to themselves. Anyway, Thomas's phone rings and he answers it. He puts it on loudspeaker so he can carry on working.

'Thomas Neale speaking.'

'Ah, glad I've caught you, Thomas. Detective Sergeant Andy Moss of the Surrey Police. Do you have a minute?'

'Yup, sure. How can I help you, Sergeant?'

'I can see what you meant when you said Tilly's father, Callum White was a wild one. Two tours of Northern Ireland, Kosovo, Sierra Leone, then he disappears for a bit, but soon emerges serving with Special Forces in Iraq and Afghanistan.'

'So, you did get clearance to get past the Official Secrets Act,' says Thomas.

'All in the course of an official police enquiry. So, you know I've got clearance, is there additional colour you can add? I can see you're pretty handy too, Colour Sergeant Neale. Fifteen years in the Paras; that's not too shabby.'

'I served my time. I think I told you that's when I met Callum. He stayed on and joined "The Regiment", getting involved in all kinds of Black Ops stuff. He was pretty unpredictable as a Para, but things got even darker with the SAS. Far too dark for my liking, anyway.'

'I see he left the Army in 2015 as WO 1 with twenty-five years' service, the last ten as a deep penetration sniper. The records show he spent six months in hospital with PTSD, but then he disappears. Any idea of his whereabouts, seeing as you're old friends?'

'If I knew the answer to that, I'd have bloody asked him where Tilly is myself!' says an exasperated Thomas. 'Sorry, I'm just really worried about her. It's not like Tilly to take off like this. Listen, I think he went freelance for a while. Got paid big bucks for doing some really shifty stuff. Can't have helped his head much. I went for a drink with him about two years ago, for old time's sake. He was acting pretty crazy. He said the Russians were after him and that he needed to go to ground. Tilly told me one day he was there, and the next he'd just disappeared. It messed the poor kid up, especially since her mother, Carla, had just died.'

'What I'd really be interested in, is what's going on in Cal's head.'

'I wouldn't presume to know that. Cal's mind has always been rather murky, even in the old days. Add to that what he's seen and done over the years, and I'd say he's pretty messed up. I've had my own mental health scars, but not a patch on old Cal. The last time I saw him; he'd just come off treatment for PTSD and alcoholism. He was on a shaky keel, but the various pills were chilling him out. They helped, but someone like him has a hell of a guilty conscience.'

'Is that why he left the SAS? Because of PTSD?'

'Actually no, he served for several more years. The Regiment loses about fifteen senior NCOs through retirement every year, so they do their best to hold onto the "golden oldies". Officers only serve for two to three years, then head back to their home regiments. So, it's really the NCOs that carry The Regiment and provide longevity. The workload and pressure are off the scale, and these guys aren't exactly 'touchy-feely' types who talk over their issues. Many self-medicate with alcohol to blot out problems.'

'So, what happened to him? What triggered him off? His record is pretty impressive, if a little thin on detail. It certainly doesn't indicate any mental health concerns.'

Thomas snorts. 'That depends on how much was redacted before you saw it.'

'Well, maybe,' replies Moss. 'So what happened? Something must have driven this decorated war veteran to turn his back on his family and shut out the world. Something bad enough to make himself homeless and potentially have a hand in what's happened to his own daughter?'

'Neither of us knows that. All we do know is what Tilly told me when he first disappeared and then shortly before she did too. Beyond that, we just don't know.'

'Okay, let's examine the possibilities,' said Moss.

Thomas sighs. 'Do you remember those girls from that school in Nigeria that were kidnapped by the Islamist group, Boko Haram?' asks Thomas. 'It was big news a few years ago. I think about a hundred of them are still missing, despite the big celebrity campaign.'

'Yes, I remember that, why?'

'Cal was involved in securing the release of some of them. Then something went wrong out in Nigeria, and that appears to have triggered a bunch of repressed stuff in his head. I'm fairly convinced it had something to do with Islam too.'

'Why d'you say that?'

'Cal has always had an interest. Even back in Iraq and Afghan in the Noughties. He wanted to get into the enemy's head and understand their motivations. He became something of an expert on Islamic culture for The Regiment. He's fluent in Arabic, is a scholar of the holy Quran and is a practicing convert. The more he learnt about it, the more he admired Islam, but also the more he became conflicted. Matilda told me the last few times she saw him, he was paranoid and believed he was being pursued by Boko Haram. He'd become more devout and gave her a hard time for what she was wearing. Matilda wanted to please him and rebuild their relationship, but maybe something went wrong.'

'Right, I think we better leave it at that. This is all conjecture. I just wanted to touch base. We've got a missing person bulletin out for Matilda and are working with the phone company to track her calls. Even with a flat battery there's a chance of tracking it these days. We're also keeping tabs on her bank records. We've put a "Person of Interest" notification out for Callum, so something should turn up. It usually does.'

'Not a chance,' says Thomas.

'Sorry, what was that?'

'Like I said when we met, Sergeant, if Callum doesn't want to be found, he won't be. This is what he does: he disappears into the background until he chooses to strike. Speak to The Regiment; he's probably the best they've ever had at it.'

'Let's try to stay optimistic. Let me know if you hear anything and I'll do likewise.'

'Yeah, sure,' sighs Thomas. 'Thanks for calling and letting me know where you're at.' He checks the screen of his phone to make sure the call is disconnected, before putting it back into his jacket. He then leans down to pick up the bag of rotting flowers. 'Which by all accounts is bloody nowhere,' he says to no one but himself.

CHAPTER EIGHT

It's Bill Robertson who figures out how we can get Lee talking. It wasn't going to be easy and would require one of the few women here with us at Brookwood to get involved. We would be asking her to do something against her every instinct: to engage in a conversation, possibly even flirtation, with a known rapist and murderer. One who is seething with seventy-five years of pent-up rage at the injustice he feels he has suffered. Not to mention, his sheer orneriness and the fact he just plain stinks.

Hedwig Margaretha Raithel is a thirty-three-year-old nurse, who served with the US Army Nursing Corps before dying of pneumonia on the 2nd of November 1918. To us, she's just Miss Hattie, a sweet, kind lady with pretty dark eyes and curly hair. She wears the long-skirted grey uniform of the American Red Cross with a matching Fedora. Miss Hattie was one of four siblings born in Farmington, Wisconsin to Bavarian immigrants, and it has been a long-standing source of irritation that her cross says she's from Colorado. Unmarried — which at the time was unusual for her age — she was dedicated to her work at the North Eastern Fever Hospital in Tottenham, London. Here, she was exposed to the second great wave of the influenza epidemic sweeping through the nation that autumn. To Miss Hattie's eternal frustration, she was taken when she might have been at her most useful. Her grave is a few rows away from mine, buried alongside a few of her sister nurses. We've been within each other's eyeline since 1918:

The conifers that grow between the American plot and the adjoining British World War One plot are oddly shaped trees. They have low, sweeping branches that look as if they are weighed down by swings. Perhaps they grow like that naturally, but my belief is that their shape is the result of the 'comely creatures' that have perched there for years, holding court among their many admirers. We have so few women buried at Brookwood Military Cemetery. Many more are commemorated on the monuments to the lost, but they have no known graves. It is only those buried here that can linger, of which there are perhaps only a dozen or so. Consequently, they are always in great demand for their conversation and company. The American nurses amongst them include Miss Hattie, Miss Florence and Miss Theresa. The pine boughs are a favourite perch from which to hold court. With so many boys craving their attention, some have become rather self-important, but not our Miss Hattie, who is sweet as pie. I've known her for a long spell, and she's always been happy to help and talk to anyone.

Bill Robertson is her favourite. There's something about the rough manners of the Scotsman with a big heart that seems to appeal. He knows she'd never refuse a request for help, particularly once he's explained why. She agrees immediately but is worried she's getting in over her head, having to deal with an odious character like Lee.

'Hattie, my darling, I know it's scary,' says Bill. 'But just remember, he cannae hurt you, even if he wanted to. It may seem frightening, but I'll not be far away. All you've got to do is holler and I'll come running!' She gives a nervous smile, nods and steels herself. 'I know it feels awfully risky, but d'you think you can handle it, darling?'

'I suppose so,' she replies dubiously.

Mack gazes up at Miss Hattie on her perch. 'What we're trying to find out, Miss Hattie, is if Lee actually knows anything about where Tilly might be.'

She reaches down to Mack and cups his face in her hands. 'What is this girl to you, my dear? Why do you want me to do this?'

'She means a great deal to me, Miss Hattie. I dinnae ken much about women, and maybe that's why I'm stuck here, but I feel the loss of her terribly. I'm all at sea and it's awfully confusing to me.'

Miss Hattie gives him a sweet smile. 'I think the key word you've just said is "feel". Now, that's not something we have the chance to do much of around here. If someone can get that reaction, surely it's precious. My brave Billy here does that for me. I recall many years of emptiness before he arrived with his dear friend Louis. Thank you for telling me. I'll do whatever I can. Now, please tell me what I've got to do.'

'I dinnae think it'll be too difficult,' says Bill. 'Just get him blethering. Louis is keeping an eye on where he and his pal are lurking and will let us know when they're on the move. If anything goes wrong, I'll be there in a flash. Young Mack'll be with me, aye?'

'Aye,' nodded Mack determinedly.

Lee and Willy's favourite hangout is what they call 'the river'. It's not much more than a rainwater culvert that runs along the southern boundary of the cemetery, parallel to the parade of giant Redwoods called the Long Avenue. The two of them like to stand in the water, just a few feet deep, irrespective of the weather, because of course the cold doesn't bother us at all. Willy likes it by the water; he says it reminds him of home in Ironton by the banks of the Ohio. He often tells Lee about the parties he used to go to, getting the local gals drunk and having some fun.

'Well, hi there, boys. I thought I was the only one who likes to paddle down here. Mind if I join you?' asks Miss Hattie. 'Say, son, how about you giving a lady a hand down?'

Lee looks up. 'Where'd you come from, lady?' he asks gruffly. 'I know you can't be from the South.'

She smiles and takes off her hat to reveal curly hair tucked up in a tidy bun at the back of her head. 'Nope, I'm from Farmington, Wisconsin. You ever heard of it?'

'No ma'am,' he replies in his rope-burned voice. 'I don't suppose there's too many Black fellers up there?'

'Nope, none. Mostly German and some Irish folks.'

'German, huh? Them's who we were fighting in my war. Them, the Italians and the Japanese,' says Lee. 'Never did get no chance to get stuck in, though.'

'Well, I suppose you're lucky then,' replies Miss Hattie. 'We were fighting the Germans in my war too, but I'm a nurse, and my job is to take care of the boys, no matter where they're from. We all suffer the same. D'you see what I'm saying, boys?'

'Yes, ma'am,' the pair reply together.

'And what might your names be, gentlemen?' she asks.

'I'm Lee Davis, ma'am. This here's William Harrison Jr.'

Willy takes off his Army Air Corps cap and nods his head. 'Howdy.'

'Nice to meet you. I'm surprised I haven't seen you around. I've been here a long time. More than a hundred years, would you believe? In all that time, things don't seem to have changed that much. The world just rearranges itself now and then, and gets started on another damned fool war and more folks get killed. That's the tragedy of being stuck here; we see it all happen but are powerless to change anything. Eternal witnesses to the folly of human nature. Don't you agree, boys?'

'I wouldn't rightly know, ma'am,' says Lee. 'I've been angry for the longest time. I know I've done wrong for being so angry, but there ain't nothing I can do to change that. I planned to achieve so much, but everything was stacked against me and went wrong. I can't change anything, but I sure as hell ain't gonna be pushed around no more. People talk about what I've done, but what about what was done to me? What about what I lost? No one cares about that. It's like I just don't matter.'

Miss Hattie takes a seat on the bank. 'I can't say I know exactly what you're referring to, Lee, but I don't think it matters anymore. We're all dead and forgotten, but for some reason a bunch of us are still here. It doesn't really matter why. What does matter, I believe, is that we are good to one another to make our time tolerable, and if we can help those that still live, surely we have that duty. That way, maybe we can share what we learnt during our own short lives. Maybe that way we can earn our way out of here?'

'You got something to regret in your life, ma'am?'

'Well, I surely must have, or I wouldn't still be here now, would I? We've all got our cross to bear, Lee. It doesn't matter what it is. Gotta try to be the best we can and help those that can still be helped. Don't y'all agree?' The pair nodded bashfully. 'Well then, boys, let's see if we can't help each other. How about y'all tell me what you know about that sweet child Tilly?'

'You better follow us,' says Lee, and I creep along behind them as they lead Miss Hattie away to a secluded spot.

'Why aye, what are you two doing here again? Ye know this is wor spot,' seethes Oscar Brown as soon as he sees them. 'Everybody knows to keep out of wor way and I'll keep out of yours,' he rages. 'And who are you bringing doon now?'

He peers out from the concrete drainage pipe that pours muddy rainwater into the culvert at the boundary of the cemetery. This is his refuge, inside the dark damp tube that smells of rotting weed and dead fishy things. It is his private place, away from the scores of visitors.

Growing up in Hexham in Northumberland, Oscar went down Fallowfield pit like everybody else, but even as a lad, he preferred working alone, handling the blasting caps, fuse wires and explosives, rather than being part of a pit gang. Oscar's work was deemed vital for the war effort, so he needn't have gone when the call-ups went out, but then the lasses with the white feathers in the town started singling him out. They didn't care that mineworkers were exempt from the draft. Once they started picking on his wife Rosie at the glove factory, he knew he'd have to bow to the inevitable. It was tough, mind, leaving the family and even old Maggie, Rosie's mam, who cared for the bairns while they both worked.

Oscar reported to the Barrack Road drill hall in Newcastle upon Tyne, headquarters of the 1st Northumbrian Brigade, Royal Field Artillery. By May 1916, he was in France serving King and Country, but hadn't had much military training at all. He was put straight to work, doing pretty much what he'd done before, working with explosives. That summer, Oscar feverishly prepared four of the nineteen landmines that had secretly been dug by Royal Engineer tunnellers beneath the chalky soil of the Somme department of northern France. Several tons of Amotal high explosives were packed deep, then connected to miles of blasting wire set by canny artillerymen like Oscar. Rigged for firing on the morning of Saturday, 1st July 1916, they would together create the largest manmade explosion in recorded history, marking the start of mankind's deadliest battle at the Somme. It would rage for a hundred and forty-one days, with an estimated 630,000 British casualties and 660,000 German deaths for little discernible gain by either side.

Oscar's memory of that time was confused. He could only recollect two moments, one distinctly more pleasurable than the other, but both, in their own way, were equally devastating. His unit was part the 50th Northumbrian Division stationed on the outskirts of Amiens. During the preparations for the battle, men and equipment amassed in the area, leaving no doubt that something big was afoot. They were given hot food, new uniforms and weapons, and even bathing facilities were laid on, all of which didn't bode terribly well. In the tense atmosphere, men were desperate to blow off steam before the meat-grinder started up again, so when evening passes were offered, they were snatched up enthusiastically. Oscar was quite shy and generally kept to himself, but the Geordie tunnellers he'd befriended insisted that he come along to sample the delights of wine, women and song that Amiens might offer. The night soon became a blur, involving a lot of red wine and cognac, neither of which he'd drunk before, and then some wild carousing. Inevitably, he ended up in the arms of a pungent dark-haired *demoiselle* with a tantalising black birthmark on the soft, pale skin of her neck. She smelt of cigarettes, cheap cologne and sweat, but took good care of *son petit Tommy*, then proceeded to empty his wallet. Back at camp with his gang of jolly Geordie lads, Oscar was broke but in high spirits, singing along with their raucous songs.

His other memory was of the opening explosions to the battle of the Somme. His eardrums burst, even deep as he was in his underground refuge. The result was debilitating deafness for several weeks. When he came up to the surface, all he could see was shell-strewn devastation. The place was littered with bully-tins, smashed equipment and fluttering scraps of tattered uniforms hanging on the wire. In misty, hollow pockets were the tangled remains of bodies, as if left behind by some crimson tide that had quenched the scorched earth. Shattered timbers, tangled barbed wire and the gnarled skeletons of blasted trees scratched at him as he staggered forward, his balance completely lost. Before him, the devastation was everchanging and yet somehow horrendously uniform. In the days that followed, he numbly took part in several attacks and counterattacks, but only became fully aware of where he was several weeks later.

Brookwood Hospital and Asylum at Knaphill in Surrey was as foreign a place to Oscar as France had been. Once there, it was like a slow parting of dense, dark clouds as he returned bit by bit to the land of the living. His first recollection there was looking down at himself and being surprised at what he was wearing. For a start, he was clean, dressed in blue rather than khaki and had his right arm in plaster. The hem of his blue flannel trousers were bell-bottomed like a sailor's, with huge white turn-ups. On his feet were tweed slippers over stockinged feet, which he knew was unusual as he'd never worn slippers in his life.

Looking up from his armchair, he saw a kind-faced woman holding a glass of water. She smiled at him and checked his pulse. She wore a long white dress under a wraparound apron with a large red cross on it, and on her head was a prim white bonnet. She was talking, but he couldn't hear a word. She seemed surprised when he indicated he was deaf, but her hands were soft, and she smelt deliciously of soap. He assumed she was a nurse and mouthed, 'Where the devil am I?' but got no answer.

His hearing gradually improved, and he pieced together that he was at Brookwood Hospital, in a village called Knaphill in Surrey. He'd apparently arrived with a badly broken arm, unresponsive and what the Cockney hospital porter described as 'proper bomb-happy.' Mute and catatonic for several weeks, he uttered not a word, nor was there any reaction to his surroundings. At nighttime, he'd have terrible nightmares, screaming and raging, alarming the others in the ward as he tried to escape unknown terrors. His hands shook uncontrollably, and sometimes he would stare vacantly at nothing at all, with what the earnest young ward doctor described as 'the thousand-yard stare.' Physical wounds began to mend, but the deeper mental ones were more concerning.

On New Year of 1917, Oscar was still a patient at Brookwood Hospital, despairing over whether he would ever recover. He counted himself lucky compared to the mutilated, or the severe mental breakdowns brought about by the horrors of war. There was some good news in the spring, providing a cause for optimism. It was a letter from Rosie telling him that after her conjugal visit to the asylum's married quarters he was going to be a dad again. The news coincided with confirmation that he would officially be invalided out of the Army and put forward for a disability pension. In the meantime, his place at Brookwood Hospital was secure and he became a trustee patient, helping to provide care for other patients, both military and civilian.

One day, one of the asylum's senior physicians, Doctor Ogilvy, came to examine him.

'I see you've got quite a rash on the palms of your hands and a curious sore in your hairline. I'd like to take a closer look at that.' He ran his fingers through Oscar's hair and asked, 'When you were in France, Mister Brown, were you wounded by any fragments to your skull?'

'Not that I know of, sir. I had a badly broken arm, was deaf as a post, and one doctor said I had "combat neurosis", but Jocky the porter said I was just "bomb-happy".'

'I see,' said Doctor Ogilvy. 'Could you hold out your hands, palms-up, please? Now, pop your mouth open, so I can have a quick look.' Oscar did as he asked but began to feel a little uneasy. 'Have you had sore gums over the last few weeks or months?'

'Sometimes, but to be honest, sir, my teeth have never been great. What's this all about? I've bumped me head sorting out one of the boisterous lads, but otherwise I'm bonny and fit.'

'Yes, well, I may have to do some more tests, and I know this may come as a shock, Oscar, but I fear you may be suffering from secondary syphilis. In fact, those sores in your hair are actually an early sign of the tertiary phase of the infection. I'm terribly sorry.'

'Sy-phi-lus. I'm sorry, doctor, but what does that mean?' asked a bewildered Oscar.

'Well, sometimes it's called "the French disease", but you'll know it as VD or the clap.'

'Oh my God, the clap! But how?'

'I think you're best placed to answer that, but I suspect you contracted it whilst you were in France.'

'Can it be treated? Will I recover?'

'Well, it's difficult to say without further tests, but I'm afraid you're getting towards the advanced end of the diagnosis. I suspect your mental affliction when your first came to us may have masked the earlier symptoms. There are treatments, of course, which can help, but I'm afraid they involve mercury and can be really quite unpleasant.'

'I cannae believe it…'

'I'm very sorry, Oscar, but in some ways, you're fortunate to be in an institution like ours, used to treating mental issues linked to syphilitic infection. I'm afraid military hospitals usually take a dim view of venereal infection, deeming it somehow a self-inflicted injury.'

Oscar's prognosis did not improve. In a time before penicillin and antibiotics, treatment for syphilis was drastic and agonising. The symptoms, once at an advanced stage, were relentless and ultimately fatal. For Oscar, the fear and pain over the next two years were hard to live with, but it was the associated embarrassment and shame that wounded him to the core. His Rosie refused to have anything more to do with him, especially when the bairn was born weak and sickly, and when her teeth came in, they were pointed like those of a pike fish.

His health deteriorated and the sores in the bone of his skull spread. His decline was pitiful and he began to suffer from dementia and violent manic episodes. By May 1919, Britain was at peace again, but Oscar Brown died, demented and raving. By then, most of his nose and face had been eaten away by the bacteria that he'd caught from a 'mademoiselle from Armentières'. He found little peace in his grave:

836164 GUNNER

O. A. BROWN

ROYAL FIELD ARTILLERY

20 MAY 1919

HE FOUGHT THE GOOD FIGHT

'The lass is mine, ye cannae have her!' screeches Oscar now, driving Miss Hattie, Willy and Lee back up the riverbank with the force of his fury. They all know of 'Crazy O,' the most tortured and unpredictable of the dark wraiths that exist on the periphery of Brookwood.

'Howay wi' ye. She's not as bonny anymore, but wor lass is still mine,' Oscar mumbles defiantly, although they've already gone. I step out from where I was concealed. 'Here comes the chief,' Oscar says. 'Why can you people not leave us alone? Me and the lass are not doing any harm. Just leave us be, Mouse. She's mine.'

'Well now, she's not, is she, Oscar?'

'She came tae me for protection.'

'No, Oscar, she didn't. She's got her own people; they're worried and looking for her. You're not making things better.'

'She's safe with me, man. I'm taking care of her.'

'I'm sorry, Oscar, but you're not. How can having her rot down a filthy drainpipe be taking care of her? She deserves better than that. Please let me see her, Oscar.'

He's silent, brooding and twitching, then unexpectedly he scrambles from the mouth of the pipe. 'Just you, Mouse. None of them busybodies, them filthy murderers and kiddie fiddlers.' Catching sight of Lee and Willy again, he screeches, 'I heard what you said when you found her! I heard what you said you wanted to do if you could. Bloody perverts, showing no respect for the poor lass.'

He lets me pass, hunched over like a monstrous crab scuttling around in its lair. I crouch low to crawl into the dank pipe. In life, this would have been a terrible ordeal, since I've never been too good with small spaces. This is cold, dark and wet, and it stinks of putrid corruption. None of it can affect me now, but that don't mean I ain't squeamish or just plain scared. The sleeves and knees of my uniform scrape along the rough concrete inside the pipe. It's half-filled with muddy water and leads to a sort of anteroom with a metal inspection hatch in the roof. Floating in the water, I can see Tilly, or at least what's left of her. She's been missing for a while, and I can tell she's been dead for a spell. Being half-submerged has undoubtedly speeded things along. I've seen more than my fair share of the dead, and what lies before me is sadly far too familiar.

Tilly's fine features are gone. Her body is already past the bloating phase of decay, although her limbs below the surface are water-logged. Decomposition and putrefaction are almost complete, and yet the stink in that confined space is unbearable. Fluid has drained away from her exposed face and the soft tissues, skin, flesh and cartilage have withered. It is only the dark halo of her long hair spreading like seaweed through the water that identifies her. That and her black clothing, contrasting sharply with the bright red cord wrapped tightly around her ankles, wrists and throat.

Oscar is telling me how beautiful his Ophelia is, but I'm struggling to see anything resembling what he describes. I start to gag, not from horror but at the sheer heartbreak of discovering the fate of our Tilly. Oscar is crooning now, gently touching her ravaged face as clumps of hair fall away in the dank water. I can't stand it; I have to get out.

Emerging bankside, the others crowd towards me, full of questions and demands. My faithful old pal, big-hearted Taddy, sees the anguish on my face and pushes them away to give me space to catch my breath and control my emotions.

'Give him a second, please, my friends,' he says, holding up his hands to stop the torrent of well-meaning questions. I try to compose myself but take too long for Mack. He makes a dash for the pipe. His cry of despair from within the earthen bank jolts me out of my numb dismay.

I will never forget the shock and anger on my friends' faces. The boy's muffled sobs harden my resolve. This cannot go unpunished. 'Someone knew what they were doing and did this to our Tilly,' I say. 'We're going to find out who and make them pay.'

My words silence the group. I see several nod, still horrified by what they've learnt. Lee and Willy are skulking at the back, unusually quiet and contrite. Taddy and Miss Hattie cross themselves and whisper a prayer, one in Polish, the other in her soft American accent, concluding together, '*In nomine Patris, et Filii et Spiritus Sancti. Amen.*' Standing by his beloved Hattie, gruff old Bill has his head bowed and a comforting arm around her. Both he and his best friend Louis have tears in their eyes. It is a heart-breaking sight to see grown men cry.

I try to swallow the catch in my throat. 'We need to let Thomas know. There won't be much left of the poor child if we don't act quickly.'

I look at Taddy, my dearest friend, who is trying to comfort a sobbing Mack. He catches my eye and nods. I know he's thinking what I'm thinking. Our only hope is Luke. Only he can see and hear us, but how can we possibly make him understand something as dark and horrific as this? How can we tell him something that will break his heart?

CHAPTER NINE

Remembrance Sunday is the biggest day of commemoration in military cemeteries across the country and Brookwood is no exception. The usual suspects turn up, the British Legion, the Scouts, local clergy and dignitaries, veterans and flag bearers, and also many school children who swell the numbers and the volume. The grounds are carpeted with red paper poppies, artificial wreaths and a multitude of little wooden crosses scrawled with inscriptions like, *To Great Uncle Bert. Lost in Normandy, July 1944. Gone but never forgotten.*

As Brookwood's head groundsman, Thomas wears a blazer and his regimental tie. Luke is beside him, dressed up in a jacket. I hear them asking about Tilly, saying she would surely never miss a Remembrance Sunday, and my heart breaks for them. I need to help them find her body and bring her to rest, but I haven't worked out how to communicate that awful message through Luke.

The crowds have thinned by mid-afternoon, and only Commonwealth War Graves Commission staff and a few hangers-on are left. I have gathered as many of the other Brookwood Boys around me as possible and as Luke and Thomas wander over to the American Cemetery, I signal to everyone to gather around Luke. I hope he will be able to sense us.

Pressing close are Taddy and I and several others, including Miss Hattie, Bill, Mack and Louis. We move closer, but he doesn't react. We're yelling and hollering, trying to get through to him, but he ain't responding. I try passing through him and

I think I notice him stiffen, but he doesn't say anything to Thomas. I'm getting mighty frustrated. Then, suddenly, Taddy begins to sing. At first nothing happens, but I notice Luke's eyes appear to glaze over. Taddy keeps going. He's singing in French. It's an opera song I recognise but I don't know the words.

Unexpectedly, Luke takes a deep breath and begins to sing along, also in fluent French:

'*Et maintenant écoutez ma chanson!*
Pale et blonde dors sous l'eau profonde,
La, Willis au regard de feu!
Que Dieu garde celui qui s'attarde dans la nuit au bord du Lac bleu!'

'Luke! What are you doing?' asks an alarmed Thomas.

Juliet has joined them, and she stops to listen to Luke. 'He's singing Ophelia's aria from Ambroise Thomas's *Hamlet*,' she tells Thomas. 'It's my absolute favourite. This is the part usually sung by a soprano, but your son is a remarkably fine countertenor. I had no idea he was so good.'

'He's not,' splutters Thomas. 'He just likes to sing.'

'When did he learn to speak French?' she asks, incredulous.

'He hasn't. What's he saying?'

Juliet listens, then quickly translates.

Luke begins walking towards the culverted stream along the southern limit of the cemetery. Behind him, he's trailed by a small party of the living, and also the dead.

Approaching a manhole cover he suddenly stops, his arms dropping by his sides. I know that beneath it, poor Tilly is snagged. I start gesticulating, miming as if I'm trying to lift the lid, but I can't tell if Luke can see me. He keeps singing:

'*Sous les flots endormi,*
Ah, pour toujours, adieu, mon doux ami! Ah, cher époux, ah, cher amant!'

Ah, doux aveu! Ah, tendre serment! Bonheur supreme!
Ah, cruel, je t'aime! Ah, cruel, tu voix mes pleurs! Pour toi je meurs.'

Juliet explains, 'This is the part when Ophelia goes mad and drowns herself, believing Hamlet has abandoned her.' She quickly translates what Luke has just sung, but it takes Thomas a little while to get the gist.

He turns abruptly and runs over to a locked tool bin that is nearby. He reaches into his pocket to retrieve a bundle of keys and selects the right one for the padlock. He returns with a manhole cover tool and a powerful torch. Checking manholes is a routine maintenance task for his team, perhaps a little overdue given the recent rains, so it doesn't take him long to get it open.

Even before he shines his torch into the darkness, I can see that Thomas knows there's something dead down there. Beside him, Juliet cries, 'Oh my God!' and begins to retch. She reaches for Luke protectively while trying to stop herself from being sick. 'Come with me, Luke. Let's stand back while your dad takes a look.'

Steeling himself, Thomas shines the light down the hole to reveal the shape of a body, dressed entirely in black, featureless but for a halo of dark hair. The blood drains from his face and he closes the manhole lid. He turns grim-faced to Juliet. 'You'd better call the police.'

She lets go of Luke's hand, who steps towards his father.

'Don't look, son. I'm afraid it's Tilly down there.'

Luke is no longer singing. He is moaning, clutching his head and looks desolate. 'I know,' he manages. 'The Brookwood boys told me.' And then he collapses.

Tilly's ashes are scattered at Brookwood on a foggy Christmas Eve. Her cremation took place this morning at Woking Crematorium with a small gathering, mainly colleagues from Halstead Prep school where she worked and some school and college friends. There were also representatives of Surrey Police, a few CWGC personnel and a couple of local journalists sniffing for a story. Thomas and Luke were the only 'family' present.

This evening the fog lies thick, lending a more eerie atmosphere to the ceremony than was intended, the pale rows of headstones seeming half-buried as if in snowdrifts. Unheard by the living, the Shrieker finds the perfect moment to give a mournful cry. Considering it is Christmas eve, it is quite a crowded affair, but of course only half the attendees are visible to the living eye. Luke scatters the grey dust, which settles on the dewy lawn before the Monument to the Missing, Tilly's favourite spot.

Unprompted, Luke starts to sing a haunting version of 'Silent Night'. By the time he's finished, there isn't a dry eye on either side of the mortal veil.

When Tilly first appears amongst us, she's in the state we found her in. It's not uncommon for newcomers to arrive injured, taking a while to recover. It's just a question of time, and that's not something we're ever short of in our little world.

I recognise her straight away, despite the damage to her face. She can't speak, indicating the red cord that is still tight around her neck. I take her hand in mine.

'You're gonna be fine, Tilly. Old Mouse will take care of you. You've got plenty of friends around here, more than you'll ever know. I know all this is bewildering, but please believe me, you've nothing to be scared or sad about.'

When she first becomes aware of her surroundings, Tilly struggles to see clearly. When she does manage to focus, she sees a kind-looking man smiling down at her. She can't speak and feels very strange, sort of bloated and oddly stiff. Somehow, she isn't frightened and strangely, she feels safer than she has in a long time. Somehow, she knows she isn't alone.

The man is about the same age as her father and speaks in a drawling accent. He introduces himself as Mouse. 'Please don't fret, you hear? Old Mouse has got you.'

She tries to answer through the terrible tightness at her throat. She touches it gingerly, feeling a taut roughness that triggers a flash of memory that chills her through. She doesn't want to remember that but is grateful there is no more pain. Strangely, she finds she is not struggling to breathe despite the restriction around her neck. Bewildered, she glances at her hands, horrified at their pale, bloated state. With rising panic, she looks up into the reassuring eyes of the man called Mouse.

'Don't worry about that, Miss Tilly. You're gonna feel a mite strange for a spell, but it'll pass.' He helps her to sit up, then rise unsteadily to her feet. She looks around and the surroundings seem familiar. The wooden benches beside the gate, the Stars and Stripes on the tall flagpole, hanging limply in the mist. Above it, she knows there is a bald eagle painted gold, indistinct in the darkness and low cloud. The atmosphere is sombre and melancholy, but so familiar; it is her Brookwood.

Two men step through the swirling mist. Tilly is struck by how handsome they are. Mouse claps the younger one on the shoulder. He is in a uniform like her father used to wear. 'This is David; we call him Mack. He's from Scotland and is kinda shy.'

'Nice to meet you, ah … Miss Tilly. David McMurray of the Coldstream Guards,' he says rather formally, then instantly reddens. Tilly finds it endearing. Mack glances at Mouse nervously, who chuckles.

'Yup, Mack's been real keen to meet you, Miss Tilly.'

The lad's cheeks are crimson now, and he shuffles his feet as Tilly tries to smile.

'This here is my good friend, Tadeusz.'

The second soldier steps forward, clicks his heels and bows his head. He takes her hand and kisses it. She feels embarrassed, but he seems unperturbed. The young soldier bristles at the suaveness of his elder, and she's surprised by how flattered that makes her feel.

'My respects, *Mademoiselle Matilde*. My name is Tadeusz Lubelski, and I am entirely at your service. If there is anything I can do, please let me know.' He glances at his glowering companion, chuckles then adds, 'I am here only to assist Mack, and of course Mouse, in any way that may be useful.'

The younger man's face softens, and he looks embarrassed again.

'Now, boys, you hush up and give the lady some space,' says a woman with an American accent. She has a beaming smile. 'These boys do make such a fuss when a gal joins the party. You can't think straight with them all hissing at each other like tomcats. Hi there, darling, I'm Hattie, and I'll be pleased to help too. My advice is to take your time and you'll feel better soon enough. Get yourself one of these dear boys to keep you company. My own choice is that gruff old Scotsman over there. He don't look like much, but he's got a heart of gold. Say hello to the lady, Billy.'

A large man in a leather jerkin removes his green beret. 'Hullo there, lassie. Welcome.'

A small crowd has gathered around, all dressed in uniforms of different eras. To Tilly, it seems like some strange fancy dress party. Mouse offers her his arm to steady her wobbling steps. 'There is one thing to do before you settle in, Miss Tilly. Now listen, can you hear that?'

She can hear the sweet sound of a boy singing.

'*Silent night, Holy night…*'

She tightens her grip on Mouse's arm, struggling towards the voice she knows is Luke's.

'*All is calm, All is bright…*'

She wants to go to him, but Mouse holds her back. 'Not yet, Miss Tilly. Not when you're like this. He wouldn't understand. You'll see him again, I promise.'

Luke's song is beautiful and transports her to happier times. She's confused, though. Surely it can't be Christmas yet. Her memory is full of dark, terrifying gaps.

Luke walks towards them now. He stops a short distance away and she calls his name. He hesitates for an instant, then follows his father out of the cemetery.

Matilda Carla Elisabetta White was born at the Royal Surrey County Hospital in Guildford on the 19th of May 1999. Not for the first time, her Italian mother was on her own; her husband Callum was on deployment with 1 PARA in Kosovo. At the moment Tilly was born, 13:33, he and the rest of the sniper squad were tracking a detachment of Serbian troops withdrawing in compliance with a recently negotiated peace agreement. The carnage they left behind was anything but peaceful. Dozens, if not hundreds, of ethnic Albanian men and boys had been massacred by the Serbian Nationalists and buried in mass graves. Callum's lasting memory of his daughter's birthday was therefore the stink of decomposing corpses piled into hastily dug pits.

Callum being away in foreign climes on some grim mission or other was a frequent occurrence. He somehow managed to miss just about every significant milestone in Tilly's early life: first birthday, first tooth, first word and first steps. He received plenty of videos and countless letters from Carla, but it wasn't the same. When at home, life suddenly became vivid and exciting, and he always made a great fuss of Tilly, but she was nervous of his brusque movements, excessive loudness and the roughness of his horseplay.

As she grew older, Callum's temper and mood swings got worse. Tilly had many school friends but rarely invited any home, especially if her dad was there. She learned to put on a brave face during the short, often tense periods when he was on leave, finding some comfort in knowing life would soon return to the safety and normality of just her and her mum. Carla was always her rock and the only parent she needed.

When things weren't going well between her mum and dad, Uncle Thomas and Luke came round more often. That was when she felt she had a real family around her. They had Christmas, New Year and two summer holidays together, and these were some of her happiest memories.

Everything crumbled when her mum got sick. She'd been pale for a while and her lively Italian personality, *Vesuvio* as she called it, seemed to drain away. At first, Tilly thought it was her dad who was making her mum sad again, but it was something far worse. As Carla got sicker, Tilly saw less of Luke and Thomas, just when she needed them most. Her dad was around 'on compassionate leave' but he spent most of the time brooding, short-tempered and volatile.

Her one safe anchorage during this tumultuous period was her paternal grandmother, Lilian White, her Nanny Lil. Born and bred in London, she was a cockney girl from Brick Lane. Widowed at a young age, she'd taken Callum and his older sister away from London to the Dorset coast in the 1980s, wanting sunshine and fresh air for her children, so that they could grow healthy and strong. She was kind, but had a sharp tongue. She was a tiny, birdlike woman with dark curly hair, bent over by osteoporosis, the result of poor nutrition in her youth.

Childhood visits to the seaside to see Nanny Lil were the highlight of the school holidays. She thrilled Tilly with tales of Dougal, Callum's Scottish father, who had served with the Argyll & Sutherland Highlanders in Korea, Malaya, Hong Kong and Palestine. She was the one who first fired up Matilda's passion for history and genealogy, fuelling her fascination for the family's legend and lore. Always a bright child, Matilda did well at school, and quite early on decided she wanted to be a history teacher. Perhaps it was because she had no siblings that she was drawn to the company of children, developing a passion for forming young minds with stories from the past.

'We had such a lovely time, treated like royalty wherever we were, with parties in the sergeants' mess and delicious food. Sometimes, I didn't want to ask what I was eating, but it was exciting to try new things, especially after all the rubbish we'd had to eat during the war.' Nanny Lil loved reminiscing about life as a soldier's wife on foreign postings, such a contrast to her own East End childhood, where she'd had to endure the Blitz and the post-war slum clearances.

'My mum and dad did the best they could, but life was tough,' she'd say. 'My dad, Samuel, was an East End Jew who'd lived through the Russian pogroms. He married my mum, Florence — we called her Florrie. She was an East End Girl. I had so many brothers and sisters that just getting fed was a challenge. Not all of them made it out of childhood. Those that did have gone to America or Israel. I'm the only one who stayed on in old London.'

'Why was that, Nanny Lil?' Tilly remembered asking.

'London was our home in between postings, whatever its shortcomings. My Dougal loved it and whatever he wanted was fine by me. Of course, big as he was, he still had a weak heart.' Nanny Lil would tear up then. Tilly knew her grandfather had died of a heart attack. It was Nanny Lil's Army widow's pension that had then allowed her to escape London for the seaside.

Looking beyond Nanny Lil's parents, the family history became more confusing. Lil said, 'My grandmother, we called her Nan-Nan, was an East End matriarch, but I think she was originally from Hampshire. Her husband was another Scotsman, a red-haired fellow called Hamish Campbell. He had no fingers on his right hand, thanks to a grenade at the battle of the Hooge crater in Flanders in the First World War.' Nanny Lil's eyes shone when she described her own grandparents. 'They ran a large pub called the Ten Bells on Commercial Street in the East End. It was quite famous because of the "Jack the Ripper" murders. Some of those girls that were killed had been drinking there, but for our family it held nothing but good memories. Nine children, they had. Would you believe it? Only seven lived and the oldest was my mum, Florence.'

Nanny Lil smiled conspiratorially, as if she had a secret to reveal. 'My mum had a dark complexion compared to her ginger siblings. But after the Great War, there were so many lost fathers, grieving widows and little orphans that people didn't ask too many questions. Particularly since Nan-Nan was such a force of nature, larger than life and ruling her roost with a rod of iron.' Nanny Lil giggled. 'People still remember her down them parts and talk about the wild ragtime soirées she'd host at the Ten Bells, dancing the night away with the best of them.'

It was Nanny Lil who first speculated that her Nan-Nan might have had a first husband, or at least a feller who might be Florrie's father. She had nothing to go on, other than family stories about an ancestor lost during the Great War. Added to which, she had dim recollections of being taken by her grandmother by train to a cemetery in the countryside.

By a process of elimination, Tilly worked out that it must probably have been Brookwood, and that's how her peculiar love affair with the cemetery began. After a chaotic childhood, she felt immediately drawn to its peaceful calm and dignity, and started visiting regularly throughout her teens. After college, she found a job as a teaching assistant not too far away, and then a flat nearby. When Nanny Lil passed away, a few years after Tilly's mum, her passion intensified, and she would spend hours learning about Brookwood, uncovering the stories of those buried in the military cemetery and then also the vast civilian one.

She discovered that in Victorian Britain, London's cemeteries had reached bursting point and a solution had had to be found since the 'dearly departed' were finding their way into the capital's drinking water. More space was needed, so a plan was hatched to clear out centuries' worth of the metropolitan dead. In 1852, the London Necropolis & National Mausoleum Company was created by parliament to tackle the issue. A two-thousand-acre site was purchased at Brookwood, near Woking, just twenty-five miles from London and easily accessible from Waterloo Bridge station. In time, over a quarter of a million souls would be buried here, with Brookwood becoming the largest cemetery in western Europe. Compared to nearby Woking, with a paltry one hundred thousand inhabitants, Brookwood is a veritable city of the dead. During her childhood, growing up on various military housing barracks dotted around Surrey, Tilly had always known that Woking was pretty quiet, but had no idea that the dead had really put the town on the map.

She loved discovering the stories of the great and the good buried at Brookwood. She stared for hours at the tragedies and losses written large across the grand mausolea, the intricately carved Celtic crosses and looming Victorian funerary monstrosities. She was interested in everything, from the tiny graves of lost babies, decorated with stone teddy bears, to the garish gold-lettered black marble edifices honouring the patriarchs of Woking's Italian community, sometimes with troubling connections with *la Cosa Nostra*. It was the sheer diversity of races and religions and the complex relationships between the living and the dead that Tilly found utterly fascinating.

It was those contrasts that spoke to her most profoundly. The stark simplicity of the Ismaili Muslim plot where each grave is an identical white pentagonal headstone, with only a name, date of birth and death, compared to the grandiose Edwardian monuments, festooned with carved weeping angels, or art deco eagles, or even sarcophagi hewn from raw granite. The stories of the personalities buried here made her head spin. From Freddie Mercury, the legendary singer of Queen, allegedly with his grandparents somewhere amongst the imposing Zoroastrian mausolea of ancient Parsee design, to Saint Edward the Martyr, a Saxon King of England. Or even the scandalous socialite, Margaret Campbell, Duchess of

Argyll, whose 'headless man' divorce case was the talk of the 1950s. So many stories, so many lives, and all in this one quiet corner of Surrey.

Brookwood awakened a passion for her own family's history, with the tantalising prospect of finding the elusive long-lost ancestor that Nanny Lil had hinted at. Perhaps in trying to find this missing link, she was subconsciously trying to connect with an absentee and increasingly erratic father. When not working at school or hanging out with a few friends, she would spend time either at Brookwood or researching genealogy websites, census reports and the military records office at Kew. She began piecing together her family's history, adding colour and context to what she already knew, but still never managed to get past the barrier of her mysterious and indomitable great-great-grandmother Nan-Nan. She'd been alive from 1894 to 1959, and Tilly knew she was born in Hampshire and died in London. Her own parents had also been publicans, but beyond that Tilly could find very little.

It was Spring 2019, when Tilly decided to get her DNA tested. She reasoned that perhaps by getting a better understanding of her genetic make-up she might uncover something that might prove inciteful. It involved providing a simple saliva sample and then posting the pack off, with a three-week wait for results which she found excruciating. When an email popped into her inbox just a week later and her heart leapt, thrilled and terrified in equal measure. She worried that she might have messed up the sample, but it turned out to just be confirmation that her sample had been received and analysis was underway.

Exactly on promised schedule, a second email arrived and clicking the link, she was confronted by results, some as expected and others that were absolutely not.

Ancestry Composition

Your DNA tells the story of who you are and how you're connected to populations around the world. It traces your heritage through the centuries and uncovers clues about where your ancestors lived and when.

Here is your composition profile:

Matilda White:

Italian 39%

Sardinian 6.6%

British & Irish 36.9%

Eastern European 9.4%

Sub-Saharan African 4.7%

Native American 3%

The analysis document went on to apportion each percentage of Tilly's genealogical provenance between her parents. Her mother, Carla Fessetta's half of the results was made up of European ancestry, and her father, Callum White, contained some European, but also unexpectedly West African and Native American origins. She was completely thrown by her father's results.

Tilly's hair was dark, and she tanned easily during the summer. She'd always attributed that to her mum's Latin provenance or Nanny Lil's curly dark hair from her father's eastern European Jewish ancestry. After reading through her results, Tilly spent hours peering into a mirror, searching for the features she might attribute to one origin or another. She didn't really know what she was looking for but was pleased she'd finally found some real connection with her roots.

Clearly, the blood of many lands flowed in her veins, and with that she'd found a new kinship and sense of belonging she'd never felt before. More than ever, she was determined to find her mysterious ancestor at Brookwood. The question was how?

CHAPTER TEN

The holidays are often a lonely time for us — a time when we feel the absence of a lifetime's worth of friends and family most keenly. For the living, it is a time of kinship and rejoicing, with the prospect of rebirth and fresh possibilities in the new year. None of that exists for us, but strangely, this season, the arrival of young Tilly has brought something of that joy.

Mack's joy is obvious. His heart's desire is with him and the challenge facing the poor boy now is to get her to reciprocate his feelings. Ever the romantic, Taddy is charmed to see the love story unfolding. Seeing the youngsters smiling in each other's company provides some relief in an existence wracked with guilt for taking his own life and condemning his Betty to her lonely vigil.

Miss Hattie has someone new to fuss over now and that makes her happy. That in turn makes Bill happy, which makes Louis happy too. Poor Tilly is oblivious to her impact on us. We knew her when she was alive, but in death she has added an unexpected family dynamic to our motley clan.

Day by day, Tilly heals and grows stronger. Her smile seems more present now than in life and is a powerful tonic for the jaded amongst us.

It is a light that has touched even the darkest recesses, those we believed were beyond redemption. Take Lee and Willy, for example, long cast as pariahs for their evil deeds in life. They've been raised in the estimations of many, and despite their early taunting about Tilly 's whereabouts, their relationships with the community have changed. They continue their conversations with Miss Hattie, politer and more respectful than they ever were. She says she looks forward to their discussions, approaching them without judgement. Tilly herself met with the pair, keen to thank them for their role in easing her transition to her strange new reality.

Even the most tormented amongst us, Gunner Oscar Brown, seems calmed by Tilly. I have explained the circumstances of their time together and with remarkable fortitude for someone so young, she insisted on meeting with him. At the agreed time, I accompany her back to the culvert, calling out his name until he comes slithering from his pipe, which is still wrapped in yellow police tape, like some hissing lizard. He circles warily, quivering and twitching, failing to recognise Tilly's restored form. But there is clearly something familiar about her, something that is dear to him.

'Is that wor lass?' he croaks, his voice heavy with emotion. 'Can it be my bonny lass has come back to me? It is you, isn't it?'

'Take it easy, Oscar. Don't be frightening Miss Tilly,' I say protectively.

'Aye, Mouse, yer right, yer right. Begging your pardon, lass, old Oscar's forgotten his manners.'

'It's nice to meet you again, Oscar,' Tilly says nervously. 'And in better conditions than the last time, at least for me.' She smiles in a way that disarms him. 'I wanted to meet with you and say thank you. Everything has been so bewildering, but it's a comfort to know you were there, watching over me. Thank you.'

There are tears running from Oscar's ruined eyes. For the first time, he acknowledges that he must have been frightening. He kisses Tilly's hands, laying them on his ravaged head. The creature that has been tormented for a hundred years is soothed by the girl's gentle touch. It's strange and thrilling for me to see, and I can't help but marvel at Tilly's impact on our strange little community.

For me, Tilly's arrival has been a closing of a circle. A completion of something that I never realised had been left unfinished. I find her company entertaining; there is so much I can learn about her life and the modern world. She never ceases to surprise and delight, and has so many interests, some quite beyond an old-timer like me. She is happy to talk to anyone for hours, enthralling audiences from different eras and nations. The dead gather to listen, curious to learn about recent events in their own areas of the world. She endeavours to answer every question. Some have existed in darkness for so long, and seek her out like a source of light. She is open to any and all questions, except for anything relating to her father and the circumstances of her own demise. Tilly's impact is perhaps best illustrated by her effect on a man who was once one of the most arrogant, unrepentant and downright nasty amongst us.

At Brookwood, *Leutnant* Kurt Sidow was once considered the epitome of an unrepentant Nazi — the kind so many lying here have died fighting. He was aggressive, pompous, condescending and argumentative, and disapproved of the friendships between his comrades and their former belligerents of other nations. Despite being outranked by several *Oberleutnants* and *Hauptmanns* at Brookwood, not to mention at least three wing commanders, he maintained his 'moral high ground' as defined by the National Socialist doctrine that ruled his life. For him, all other nations were weak, morally decadent, racially inferior and simply destined to become the Reich's serfs.

By 1940, Kurt Sidow was the *Staffelkapitän* of a squadron of *Messerschmitt* Bf 110 *Zerstörers*, as well as his unit's reigning ace.

He had been leading his force of twin-engine fighters to provide close escort to serried ranks of Heinkel 111 and Dornier 17 bombers — a mass of black crosses dotted across the cloudy sky. In turn, Kurt's *Staffel* was protected by sleek single-seater Me 109Es, known as *Emils*, a fact that Kurt found particularly galling. He knew of the heavy losses amongst Bf 110s at the hands of the RAF since the beginning of the *Kanalkampf*, but he'd managed perfectly well without protection and had seven kills to prove it.

The Tommies' Spitfires and Hurricanes were undeniably faster and more manoeuvrable than the two French fighters he'd brought down during the battle for France, but he'd also killed three of the former and two of the latter since then. His aircraft's twin 20mm cannons and quad MG 17 guns had taken care of the *Englanders* and his rear-gunner Josef Repik's MG 15 had helped too. In fact, on the 18th of August, what the *Luftwaffe* had since called the 'Hardest Day', he'd bagged a brace of Tommies over Biggin Hill and Kenley, so it wasn't really such a hard day for him. Perhaps his *Kameraden* just weren't as skilled as him.

As Kurt flew out on his latest mission, his thoughts were interrupted by young Josef Repik cocking his gun and firing a quick burst into the wispy ether. Kurt did the same with the aircraft's forward-facing weapons, then waited as the rest of the *Staffel* followed suit. He then ordered them to form up in three *Schwärme*, in the 'finger four' formation and throttled up the twin Daimler-Benz engines to catch up with the bombers ahead. It was the first daylight raid on London itself, the *Führer*'s promised retaliation for the RAF daring to raid Berlin.

The bombers were in ragged Vs, tiered at different altitudes. The sheer number was humbling, crowding the sky like a swarm of locusts. Between them, sleek little Bf 109s bobbed and weaved like sheepdogs amongst a lumbering flock. Higher up, a dark formation of Bf 110s were on watch, a skulking wolfpack searching for trouble. Kurt continued his climb until his *Staffel* joined the rest of the *Zerstörer* and settled in as the 'eyes in the sky'.

A bulbous-nosed Heinkel 111 at the starboard extreme of the formation began to smoke. There was no sign of an interceptor and Kurt wondered whether it had been hit by flak. They were too high for that, so he carefully scanned the horizon. Down amongst the anxious *Emils*, the sight of the victim floundering had them swarming like agitated bees from a struck hive, desperate to identify the culprit. Some of them had yellow noses, others tails, and sometimes both. Kurt's own aircraft was long, slim and elegant with the mottled grey skin of a shark. It was un-personalised beyond the white cockerel emblem of the 9th *Staffel* on its nose, the aircraft identifier, 3U+BT, and seven victory bars on the T-shaped tail assembly.

He caught a glimmer of light reflecting off a cockpit amongst the minute, fast-moving flecks below. There were the Tommies, attacking again in their old-fashioned 'vics' and already being scattered by vengeful *Emils*. His orders were, come what may, to stay with the bombers until they reached London, unless actively engaged by enemy fighters.

In Kurt's earphones, two more bombers in trouble were pointed out. A Dornier was struggling to maintain speed and altitude, steadily falling back until it suddenly spawned four white parachutes, the crew opting to abandon their aircraft. They had a long way to fall and would be half frozen by the time they reached England's soil or perhaps the cold sea. He wished them well and offered a silent prayer for their ordeal.

'Here they come now, *Herr Leutnant*,' said Josef. 'Those cheeky *Indianer* coming out to play. There, on the portside at about four o'clock below. Rising to six thousand metres, I'd say.'

Kurt peered through his tinted goggles and could now see the enemy aircraft materialising as distinct, fast-moving dots. *Gutter Got*, that lad had great eyes. That was why he chose Josef to accompany him. It was quite unusual for a lowly *Gefreiter* to fly with a *Staffelkapitän*, but he depended on Josef's skill and eyesight, and his relentlessly positive nature. They'd been together since he'd lost Hans, his previous *Bordfunker*, killed when Kurt downed his first Spitfire back in May. How long ago was that? Only four months, yet so much had happened since then, not least four victories, largely thanks to the talented lad in the back.

Josef was a tough little Austrian, a deer hunter from the forests of Ebenthal. In contrast, Kurt was more of an urban sophisticate from Berlin. He appreciated his young comrade's directness: straight-talking when required but also correct, knowing his place. In return, Josef was devoted to his *Staffelkapitän*, who had become a bit of a father figure to him, despite sometimes being rather vain, self-centred and arrogant. For a simple country man like Josef, that was what officers and city folk were like. Aged twenty-one to Kurt's twenty-four, there weren't many years between them, but character-wise they couldn't have been further apart. They made an odd couple that somehow worked.

The young *Bordfunker* was slim with high cheekbones, topped by an unruly mop of coppery blond hair. Kurt had more corpulent, well-fed features, with closely cropped dark hair, and he was always meticulously clean-shaven. Appearances were important to Kurt. He was inordinately proud of his Iron Crosses, first and second class, and his Destroyer Clasp, displayed on his always immaculate uniform. He was perhaps a little chubby for the *beau idol* of the perfect fighter ace but was still determined to look the part.

Kurt tilted the wings of his sleek aircraft to get a clearer view of the panorama below them. There were wispy white clouds obscuring the outskirts of the city, but the muddy brown expanse of the Thames estuary was very distinctive. Beyond it lay their target: the docks. It was Tuesday, 3rd September 1940, and a perfect day for the raid, as long as enemy fighters cooperated. Some hazy beams of sunlight reflected on the water, as sooty black smudges began to appear amongst the bomber formations. The flak was inaccurate but was getting closer, a simple spin of the roulette wheel determining if you were unlucky and got struck.

'*Hahn Staffel*, Cockerel Squadron, *Staffelkapitän* here,' said Kurt into his mouthpiece. '*Indianer at* twelve o'clock level, climbing towards us.'

'*Staffelkapitän, Heinrich 8 (H for Hahn)*, more bandits at three o'clock above.'

Kurt took in the sprawl of the dirty brown city below the bombers. Sections of the drab mosaic began to flash and pulse, as dropped ordnance began exploding. Every impact was followed by a pulsing white shockwave that radiated outwards. The Surrey Quays were now visible, bound by the distinctive U-shape of the river. At twelve thousand metres, the detonations on the ground were pinpricks of light, contrasting with the massive plumes of thick black smoke already rising from blazing riverside warehouses.

'*Heinrich* leader to *Heinrich Staffel*. The eggs are dropping and *der Indianer* will soon be furious. Keep a look out, especially you, *Holzauge*,' said Kurt, addressing the spotter at the rear of the formation. 'Keep your eyes open, everybody.'

Kurt's warning was prophetic. As the *Staffel* were executing a long banking turn, a pair of speedy Spitfires sliced through the rear of the escort. The hapless *Holzauge* went spiralling out of control, leaving a trail of black smoke. More bandits appeared at five o'clock, swooping down at squadron strength from above. Kurt turned his head to check on his *Rottenhund* or wingman, who was lagging too far back for the *Schwärm's* protection.

'Watch your back, Georg! Break hard, break hard!' cried Kurt, as Josef began firing at the pursuing Spitfire, causing it to jink away from his clawing, red tracers. Georg and Emil, his *Bordfunker,* were lucky that his attack had been disrupted by Josef's fire.

'*Danke, Heinrich 1,*' panted Georg, but Kurt and Josef were already pursuing his erstwhile attacker. Pushing the throttle forward, Kurt's twin engines roared. He was hoping the retreating Spitfire wouldn't realise how close behind he was. The juddering red ring of the Revi gunsight projected onto his windscreen, gradually covering the form of his adversary. The trigger for the four machine guns in the nose and the pair of monstrous 20mm cannons beneath his pilot's seat were synchronised. As the silhouette of the Spitfire filled the ring, he pressed the trigger with a gloved hand. A solid mass of fire hosed towards the target, several 7.92mm rounds striking the slim aircraft, but the real damage came from the cannons. The twisting Spit was there one instant, and exploding into components the next. The Bf 110 punched a hole through the falling debris, as Josef shrieked, '*Horrido*!' in triumph.

'Calm yourself, Josef,' said Kurt tersely, though he was grinning beneath his oxygen mask. 'Check that Georg is back in position on our tail, and let's find the rest of the *Schwärm.*'

Far below, two Bf 110s collided spectacularly as they tried to shake off determined pursuers. Now locked in a fatal embrace, they fell in a tumbling mass of flames. A single parachute from a possible four escaped the fiery melee, but it too caught fire, spreading rapidly from silken panel to panel, until the hapless crewman fell screaming to earth. Up ahead, a large aircraft, probably a Dornier 217, began slowly spinning on its axis. Watching in silent horror, Kurt and Josef saw its huge tail fall away, broken off like a carrot. There were no parachutes this time, the bomber's fiery trail merging with the smoke rising from the burning city. Kurt realised there would be more than a few empty chairs in messes right across France tonight.

An urgent voice cried, '*Heinrich* 2 to *Heinrich* leader. I've got three Hurricanes on my tail; I could really do with some help here!' With acid wit he added, 'Don't worry, I think I've got them surrounded.'

Kurt recognised the voice of *Gefreiter* Georg Jackstadt, his *Rottenhund*, in trouble again, but at least he still has a sense of humour about it. Kurt's Destroyer dipped into a dive, spotting that his errant wingman was out of position and desperately trying to avoid the trio chasing after him like a pack of baying hounds. Emil, his rear gunner, was firing at the nearest attacker, who was closing in for the kill. Kurt swiftly lined up his own sight on the characteristic hump of the pursuing Hurricane's cockpit. In the morning sunlight, the doped fabric covering shone as if freshly oiled. He snatched the shot, but the Hurricane span away, leaving only the sparkling remains of a shattered canopy. The aircraft fell inverted, as the lumpen form of the enemy pilot tipped out of the cockpit, his parachute opening several hundred metres below them.

It was a mistake to watch their victim fall, as the second of Georg's pursuers turned on them. Tracers shrieked past as

Kurt tumbled the Bf 110, seeing flashes of brilliant white, and then felt a loud bang mid-wing. He ducked his head and pulled at the stick, feeling that he was on the verge of blacking out as blood drained from his head. Another bang brought him round as the aircraft shuddered again. They'd clearly taken a few hits, but the controls seemed to still be responsive, and he was confident he could get out of trouble.

It was his *Rottenhund's* turn to come to the rescue, keen to repay the earlier debt. Bracketed by fearsome cannon fire, the second Hurricane ran, followed by his evidently nervous wingman who was struggling to keep up. This was clearly a less experienced pilot, and Kurt was tempted by the easy kill, but with a damaged aircraft, he decided discretion was the better part of valour. Best to be cautious and head for home. In any case, two kills in one day wasn't a bad score.

'*Danke, Heinrich 2.* Do you still have me in sight?' he asked.

There was a pause as Georg scoured the sky for him. 'Ah yes, *Heinrich* 1, I can see you.'

'Excellent! Now, would you mind telling me where the hell I am?' asked Kurt mischievously, laughing with nervous relief. In his headphones he heard the entire *Hahn Staffel* join in.

'*Das ist genug,*' said Kurt finally. 'This is *Heinrich* leader; let's go home.' He set a course for Pas-de-Calais and their base at the *St. Omer Barley-Arques Aérodrome*. He was already dreaming of the glass or two of restorative red wine that he planned to enjoy. Served in a *Cristal D'Arques* glass, of course — the exquisitely delicate speciality of the region.

His thoughts were interrupted by Josef piping up from the back seat. 'Congratulations on your latest two aerial victories, *Herr Leutnant.* It is my honour to serve with you. Nine kills must surely mean the *Ritterkreuz* can't be far away.'

'We shall see, my dear Josef, we shall see,' he replied, satisfied.

The White Cockerel *Staffel* made it back to France more or less intact, unlike the rest of the III *Gruppe* or 26 *Geschwader* Wing of which they were part. Kurt's men had suffered no casualties over London with the sole exception of 3U+GT, damaged by Spitfires but able to crash-land on a French beach with the crew unscathed. Kurt's 9/ZG26 *Staffel* was rapidly developing a charmed reputation, with no losses since the beginning of what came to be known as the Battle of Britain. Surely, their luck couldn't hold, given the relentless schedule of raids thrown against the enemy, but morale remained high. Surely, the RAF must be on its knees, given the deadly toll the *Jagdflieger* were inflicting upon the Tommies.

On the 11th of September, *Hahn Staffel* flew on an escort mission for several squadrons of He 111 bombers targeting London once again. On arrival, the defensive screen of Bf 109s disappeared as they were running out of fuel. It appeared that they'd expended their reserves on *Freie Jagd* or Free Hunt whilst waiting for the bombers to arrive. The mistiming would prove costly; ten bombers were lost and *Hahn Staffel* suffered its first casualty, 3U+LT. Kurt's luck still held, though, and for his men he was becoming a talisman. On 26th September 1940, during a raid late in the day, he claimed a further Spitfire and once again the *Staffel* came through unscathed.

The next day they were over London again, but this time tasked with escorting an entire *Gruppen*. Kurt's formation was intercepted by dozens of British fighters and the day would prove murderous for the heavy wing. One of the other *Staffel* within the *Gruppe* lost twelve out of thirteen aircraft, including two experienced *Staffelkapitän* and the *Gruppenkommandeur* himself.

In the meantime, the White Cockerels claimed two Spitfires, one of them a kill in the early afternoon for Kurt, but the day's intense combat finally did take a toll on the *Staffel*. Kurt's wingmen, Georg Jackstadt and Emil Liedtke went down after a savage contest with Pilot Officer Roger Miller of No. 609 (West Riding) Squadron. It ended with a head-on collision between them, Miller's Spitfire exploding on impact and the heavier 3U+FT losing a wing and tail section before crashing to the ground. Georg was seen to parachute to safety and would spend the rest of the war in a prison camp, but his *Bordfunker*, Emil jumped too low, ending up in the tangled branches of an English oak. He died broken in a Dorchester hospital. Roger Miller was twenty years old and Emil Liedtke twenty-one.

The loss cut Kurt and Josef deeply. They felt responsible for not protecting their wingmen. Nevertheless, the *Staffel* was still comparatively unscathed, boasting the lowest casualty rate of all ZG 26, with only four aircraft and three crews lost to date. Elsewhere, losses amongst the Destroyer air fleet were catastrophic. Questions were being asked regarding whether the heavy fighters should be redeployed to another role. Like the famed Stuka Ju 87 dive bomber that had sown such terror during the *Blitzkrieg*, they seemed to be increasingly easy prey for British fighters without the cover of air superiority.

On Monday, 7th October 1940, *Hahn Staffel* were escorting more fat-tailed Ju 88 bombers of II./KG 51, targeting the Westland aircraft works at Yeovil in Somerset. Returning from the raid, they were intercepted by Spitfires of No. 609 Squadron once again. This time, their luck finally ran out. Kurt and Josef were bested by Flight Lieutenant John Dundas, No. 609's top ace with nine victories to his name. He himself would only survive a further month, during which he was awarded the Distinguished Flying Cross, his kill tally having increased to twelve. Among his kills was the *Luftwaffe's* highest scoring ace at that time, Major Helmut Wick with fifty-six victories. Dundas didn't survive to claim the plaudits for the exploit, succumbing almost immediately to Wick's vengeful *Rottenhund*, Rudolf Pflanz. *Oberleutnant* Pflanz went on to become a decorated ace himself with fifty-two victories, including an incredible forty-five Spitfires downed. In a seemingly repeating pattern, he was eventually bested on 31st July 1942.

Leutnant Kurt Sidow found little comfort in death at the hands of the British ace who had bested the great Helmut Wick himself. He raged that Dundas had received the D.F.C. for a paltry nine kills, whilst he had thirteen and no Knight's Cross. It was something that ate away at him, especially since so many of his *Jagdflieger* comrades would go on to win the coveted *Ritterkreuz*.

To make things worse, the Dummkopf Engländer even misspelt his name:

KURT

SYDOW

11.4.1916

7.10.1940

(15.B.3)

Adding insult to injury, his final mission was also the *Staffel's* last one over England. Thereafter all *Zerstörer* squadrons were redeployed as night fighters, and many of Kurt's juniors went on to become high-scoring *Experten* up against the *Terror Flieger* bombers and were hero-worshipped by the German people — a destiny that was stolen from him.

It was a thought that consumed him entirely, at a time when he should have been thinking of his lost crewmate, young Josef

Repik, killed by his side. Their graves lie a few metres apart, but Josef did not tarry. Kurt wasn't left alone, though. He was joined by the terrified and broken Emil Liedtke, his *Rottenhund's Bordfunker*, who'd fallen to his death from his burning aircraft. He was so frightened during his plummeting demise that the fear seems to have trapped him here at Brookwood; his smashed bones allow him to contort into all sorts of unnerving shapes. Liedtke and Repik lie side by side, their sparsely worded gravestones giving little indication of the very different outcomes after their deaths:

EMIL LIEDTKE
11.4.1916 – 27.9.1940
(15.A.7)

JOSEF REPIK
18.8.1919 – 7.10.1940
(15.A.8)

Kurt rages at having died too soon, before achieving the greatness that he feels was his destiny. This is epitomised by the Knight's Cross, *die Ritterkreuz*, which graces the necks of many he considers his inferiors, and that envy has consumed him for decades.

In the early years, Emil stuck to Kurt's side like a terrified dog. In time, though, he began to fade, a little every day, until he simply disappeared. This left Kurt alone, resentful at the abandonment and filled with poison.

A change occurred on the 25th of October 1983. Kurt wasn't aware that anything significant had happened. That morning, twenty-one-year-old John Basil Ramsay from Lilliput in Dorset was buried amongst us. He was born in Bombay, India, and he'd joined the RAF straight from school, serving as a ferry pilot until he converted to fighters. With only twenty-four hours of flight time in Hurricanes, he was posted to No. 151 Squadron in July 1940, based at North Weald, just as the Battle of Britain began. Pilot Officer Ramsay was listed as Missing in Action on 18th August 1940, only four weeks later.

The crash site of his downed aircraft wasn't located until August 1983, when it was found at Deal Hall Farm in the Essex marshes. With his remains was a gold signet ring engraved with his initials, JBR, a gift from his doting parents to their only son. Johnny was buried at Brookwood with full military honours, forty-three years after falling to the guns of Kurt Sidow on the evening of what the *Luftwaffe* referred to as 'The Hardest Day'.

When Johnny first appeared before Kurt, he was a slim, determined-looking young man with sad eyes and ears that stuck out a bit. He was dressed in what he'd died in: a Mae West, a leather flying cap and goggles. He smelt of the marshes where he'd lain for so long, his uniform was damp with mould. At first he mutely followed Kurt, not uttering a single word, his dark eyes full of reproach. He became Kurt's shadow, replacing Emil who had by then faded away. One day, Ramsay simply pointed at his newly engraved headstone and said, 'I forgive you.'

Kurt had no idea what this upstart *Englander* was talking about and instantly became irritated. He glanced at the stone, failing to see its significance. He didn't recognise the name, nor did he care about the engraving, which read: *One of the valiant few to whom we owe so much in proud and loving memory.* Something about the inscribed date, 18th August 1940, was familiar, though...

It came to him like a bolt of lightning. He didn't know how to react. Hesitantly, he held out his hand and for the first time shook that of his enemy. It was a small thing, but for Kurt it was the beginning of a remarkable transformation. Day by day, the pair got to know each other. All at Brookwood marvelled at the transformation of this most ardent of Nazis, now keeping company with the shy schoolboy from Dorset.

Kurt was visited a second time. At first, he only noticed the smell of something charred. It followed him until one day another young man appeared, this time with a shock of blond hair and sergeant stripes on the arms of his pale siren suit. He was wearing a grey collared sweater under it and a Mae West. His name was Sergeant J.H.M. Ellis, known as Hugh to his girlfriend and family, and as the 'Cock Sparrow' to his No. 85 Squadron mates. Despite his youth and cheeky nature, he was a blooded fighter pilot, sharing a downed Dornier 17 on 6th August 1940, damaging an Me 110 and downing a Me 109 on 18th August, and then destroying a further Do 17 on 26th August.

Hugh also fell to Kurt's guns, but on 1st September 1940, brought down in flames in an apple orchard, south of Orpington in Kent. The aircraft hit the ground so hard it burrowed ten feet into the rich earth. A booted foot and some body fragments were buried in separate graves under headstones for an 'Unknown Airman'. It wasn't until 1992 that the Hurricane was excavated, and Hugh's body was finally identified. Inside the cockpit were photos of his sweetheart Peggy and Aunt Stella in Australia. Hugh was buried alongside John Ramsay on 1st October 1993.

Leutnant Kurt Sidow now had two shadows, and in many ways, they were like different facets of his conscience. One was soft-spoken and thoughtful, the other talkative and pugnacious. They became what he called his *Kriegskinder*, his war children, and were the catalyst for Kurt's reappraisal of who and what he was. Coming face to face with youngsters that he'd killed changed Kurt Sidow forever, and our Tilly cemented that shift.

'It's so wonderful that you've found each other,' Tilly said to Kurt, John and Hugh once she'd heard their story. 'It's a joy to see you all so close.'

'*Ja, Fraulein*, but I did not make it easy,' replied Kurt. 'I was not a pleasant man.'

'What changed you?'

'My boys here,' he said. 'You see, during in the war, I was a good leader and *Staffelkapitän*, but only ever thought about myself. *Ja*, my men respected me, but if I'm honest, they didn't like me very much. You see, I was only ever interested in what they could do for me to look good. I was unable to reach certain achievements before my death, and I became angry because I thought I'd been cheated, and that it was others who had failed me. I never recognised my own shortcomings. Only now, by recognising them, have I found some peace.'

'How has that changed you?'

'Well, I lived during a time when we thought differently. I was a product of that system. With the forgiveness of my boys, my eyes have been opened. I see now that we all suffered and were led astray by our leaders. For me, the boys' forgiveness is a second chance — one I don't deserve but refuse to squander. With their help, I strive to be the best I can, and that for me is enough.'

'What d'you think you've brought to them?'

'Ach, I don't know, probably not much. Maybe a sort of father figure in a dark, frightening world for such young men. Both are barely twenty-one. Hugh has brought John out of his shell, to be less reserved and more confident. John has made Hugh more measured and less impulsive. They've become like brothers, despite being — how do you British say it? Ah, "chalk and cheese." Both were only children in life but have each other now, and *ja*, they have me.'

'Papa Kurt is being modest,' said Hugh, the more boisterous of the pair. 'He doesn't realise we both had long, lonely existences before arriving here. Finding him and then each other is a precious thing, a sort of fulfilment. You're a long time dead, and believe me, it's a lot better when you're not alone. I have a kid brother now, something I've never had.'

'Kid brother!' exclaimed John. 'I was shot down by Papa Kurt before you were, so actually that makes me older.' He grinned at Tilly. 'There's only three weeks in it.'

'Seems to me that the things that made you suffer are all gone,' said Tilly. 'You're fortunate to have found each other.' The trio nodded, made bashful by the realisation.

It took a few days before anyone realised that they hadn't seen Kurt and the boys for a while. That's how it happens, folks just disappear or fade away. They're with you and then they're not. Now, when I walk past their graves side by side, I look up at the stars and I hope they're up there somewhere. I have this fanciful idea that the stars on Orion's belt are Kurt Sidow and his boys. I find comfort in that.

CHAPTER ELEVEN

A booming rifle shot sends a flurry of panicked wood pigeons from their roosts in Brookwood's trees. It's followed by an alarmed chorus of magpies and Indian crows. Down on the ground, policemen swarm like ants from a kicked nest, their radio traffic adding to the cacophony.

'Shots fired! Shots fired!' say a dozen voices at once, the helicopter whining overhead. Amongst Brookwood's longer-term residents, the sound of gunfire is no cause for alarm. They observe the frantic policemen wryly. Most of us were soldiers in life, and with the proximity of Bisley, the sound is all too familiar. Only Tilly is alarmed, but Mack is quick to reassure her. The scene has a strange effect upon me. It's comforting, but also troubling. Tilly's presence among us is cherished, but the circumstances that brought her here remain partly unknown. There was a darkness that was revealed to me when she finally shared the tale, and now if it's possible for a spirit to be haunted himself, her story did just that to me.

It all started innocently enough. I'd taken her over to the American plot to show my unknown warrior's cross. She'd been very sweet and given me a consoling hug, after bowing her head for a moment of silence. It struck me that this was the first time anyone had ever done that, actually knowing who was down there in the soil. We walked through the adjoining First War British plot, and I recalled that when she was little, she would often spend time scouring these gravestones. There are certainly plenty of names to search, particularly at the lower end of this large plot. Here the headstones are crowded together, a confusing mass of names and regiments, all crammed together as the bodies piled high during the great influenza of 1918, a time when Brookwood struggled to cope, like it never has since.

I ask her, 'I remember you used to visit here a lot when you were a young girl. I would watch you often, scribbling down the names of dead buried here. What were you looking for? Why this particular plot?'

'Yes, I suppose I was a strange little girl,' she replies. 'Not exactly the childhood hobby you'd expect.' She laughs. 'Actually, I was looking for a long-lost ancestor. I was looking for any names that sounded familiar to my very crudely drawn family tree. As I got older, I realised how futile that was.'

'Well, you certainly spent plenty of time here. I used to watch you and wonder at the patience of this intense little girl, so focussed on her task.'

'Intense little girl,' she sighs. 'That sounds about right.'

'Let me take you to some place you probably haven't seen. It's actually why Brookwood exists at all. I'll show you the rougher parts of the cemetery, which run alongside the old railway embankment to the tracks that lead to London. I'm showing her the boundaries of our world, where discarded plastic flowers, wrapping and tattered wreaths are piled up for removal by the skip load. It isn't something most people consider, the amount of litter the dead can accumulate.

We're walking and talking when she stops in her tracks. Speaking in that still slightly lisping way of hers, she says, 'That's where I found my dad. Beside the door of that old maintenance shed.'

I look where she's pointing and see two concrete boxes cut into the slope of the embankment, each capable of holding perhaps four men apiece. They lean together because of subsidence in the soil. I'm not sure of their original purpose;

perhaps they were tool stores, junction boxes or shelters for railway navvies when the line was being built. Now, they're completely overgrown with prickly brambles, ever-optimistic birch saplings and an accumulation of mouldy leaf litter. Deserted and abandoned, the door of one is ajar and the thicket of brambles is flattened. There's a strong smell of cold wood ash from within. A casual observer would not have noticed, so strong is the odour of passing trains — a pungent combination of clogged lavatories and diesel fumes.

'He was in there, hiding like a scared animal,' she says. 'It took several visits before he even recognised me. When he did, he called me Carla, my mother's name, then cried for an hour.' Her eyes are filled with tears.

'Hush now,' I say. 'You don't need to talk about it if it hurts.'

'I need to, Mouse. There may still be time to stop him. I'm so afraid of what he's capable of. I couldn't forgive myself if he hurt anybody else…'

'Take your time, sweetheart. Just take your time.'

She balances on the uneven ground amongst the scratchy brambles, but of course they don't catch on us as we make our way in. Doing my best to follow, I glance about the hut, which smells a bit like an animal's lair. On the moss-green concrete floor is a wet khaki sleeping bag and several sealed plastic bags, containing I daren't ask what.

'He'd been sleeping rough for weeks. Here, but also in dozens of other hides around the cemetery grounds. He told me he'd never stayed in one place for more than a few nights because "they" were after him. When I asked who, he called them *Boko Haram*.'

'Who might they be?'

'They're a terrorist group from Nigeria. I believe my father was fighting there with the British Army.'

'D'you really think they'd come this far to find him?'

'No, Mouse,' she says dismissively. 'I think it's all in his head.' She closes her eyes and takes a deep breath. 'My father was a paratrooper, like Thomas. The two of them were inseparable in the Army. Our families were close, but then the two of them fell out just before my mum got sick. Dad was a bit "war crazy", and then he just disappeared for a few years whilst I was at college. When he reappeared, he was in and out of a psychiatric hospital, suffering from what you might call shellshock.'

'Shellshock? Sure, I know about that. We've got a whole lot of that around here. Everyone from Crazy O to your Mack has been touched one way or another. Maybe there's something about that trauma that's keeping so many of us here.'

'I hadn't seen him for years,' she went on. 'Then, out of the blue, I get a note at the school where I work.' Her hands are trembling, and she swallows hard. 'Where I worked, I mean.' She pauses. 'The note didn't make much sense and was barely legible. It spoke of "the wrath of a vengeful God" and "smiting down the Kuffar." I was scared but recognised the handwriting, knowing immediately it was from my father. He said he was sheltering "where proud warriors sleep" and that only they could keep him safe from "the darkness that seeks to stop my divine mission."'

'Divine mission? What on earth could that be?'

'I didn't know, but I was really frightened. I know what he's capable of. To me, it seemed like he couldn't separate fact from fantasy. What he did remember was how keen I was on Brookwood and deep down, perhaps he hoped I'd come to find him. And that's exactly what I did. I was just too predictable.'

'What did you talk about when you met?'

'I saw him a few times over several weeks. I always had to search for him, as he was constantly on the move.'

'Yes, we saw you. We couldn't understand what you were looking for. We never saw him though, he must be very good at hiding.'

'He is, one of the best. At first, he thought I was my mother, but he eventually recognised me. He was in a poor state, very skinny and not taking his medication. He was unwashed and damp and smelt of alcohol. He had a silver hip flask, which never left his side. I remember thinking it was the only clean and shiny thing about him. I think it was a retirement gift from "The Regiment".'

'What's this regiment? What did he do for them? And I guess more to the point what did they do to him?'

'My father was a sniper. A expert marksman with a rifle. I've been told he's one of the best, trained in the Parachute Regiment, but eventually recruited to the SAS, the Special Air Service, who call themselves "The Regiment".' You see, snipers are specially selected and trained in advanced marksmanship and fieldcraft. That's how Thomas and Dad first became friends. They were both selected as young paratroopers and paired up. Their job to support operations and engage targets at a distance. Working together, as shooter and observer, their roles were interchangeable, and they kept each other grounded, focussed, disciplined and sane, especially during the long hours spent immobile and unseen in hostile environments. They served several tours together, in Northern Ireland, Kosovo, Sierra Leone, the First Gulf War, then Iraq and Afghanistan. Thomas left the service, and Dad stayed on, serving with Special Forces in Iraq and Afghanistan.'

'Special Forces, what does that involve?'

She shrugs and looks forlorn. 'To be honest, I don't know. It was all top secret and certainly not the kind of stuff he'd share with his daughter. All I know is, every time he came back, he was more manic, more frightening and seemed more affected by the things he'd seen.'

'Things like what?' I asked, not wanting to be cruel, but trying to understand.

'Dad never told me, but Thomas shared the little he knew. It appears that after an incident in Nigeria, where I think some girls were killed, Dad blamed himself. He left the SAS and according to Thomas went "freelance" for a while. He apparently got paid a lot of money for doing some really shifty stuff. That can't have helped the state of his head, and I know he started drinking heavily.' She covers her eyes with her hands trying to subconsciously blot out the memories. 'He'd always been a drinker, especially after Mum died, but after the hospital stay, he'd quit for a bit. Obviously, he'd fallen into it once again.' She looks sad. 'What was odd to watch was how when he talked about his drinking, it was like watching two sides of his personality arguing. One was the gruff soldier that needed a drink to get through life, the other condescending and sneering, calling himself weak, a failure, an unbeliever.'

'Maybe the voices are in his head. It can happen. I know it's not the same, but I can still hear the screaming of my mules in the darkness of the night. It still fills me with such sorrow, dread and absolute fury. But I'm sorry, I'm interrupting. Please go on.'

'When he was calm, he came to recognise me, and we began talking almost normally. He said he was sorry and that he'd been a terrible father. He begged for my forgiveness, all the while saying he was unworthy of it.' Her voice hardens again. 'Then he would just snap and change. Right there before my eyes, suddenly angry and raging against himself, against the world and against me. He grabbed me more than once, shook me and slapped me several times, calling me a harlot. He said I was impure, unchaste and that I dressed provocatively, shaming him as a father. He demanded that I cover my hair and wear only dark clothes to preserve my modesty. "If you dress to titillate," he said, "you shouldn't be surprised if God punishes you. I have seen His vengeance on the impure and unchaste. I've seen what happens to those who get educated beyond their sex. In Nigeria, if those girls had only remained demure and quiet, perhaps they might have lived. Perhaps I could have saved them.'"

Her voice is now a whisper. 'I was to follow his commands for my own safety. He said he couldn't protect me all the time, since he needed to serve as God's punisher, the chosen axe. I got so frightened that for a while I did as he asked, but I soon started to feel angry about it. How dare he come back into my life, after being so absent, and start ordering me around? He was mentally unwell, but that gave him no right to make demands of me.' She seems to be steeling herself for what I fear will be the worst part of the tale. 'I hadn't seen him for a few weeks, but the more I thought of it, the angrier I got. I was determined to confront him and started searching all the places he'd been before. I worried, too, that his health would be deteriorating in the worsening weather.

'When I finally did find him, he was down by the culvert beyond the avenue of Redwoods. He was now very skinny and ranting. He was standing in the water, bare-chested and reciting some kind of scripture. In his hands he held green branches, tied together with a red cord. Every time he quoted a line out loud, he would swing the branches, lashing them against his bare back. He'd been at it for a while and his torso was awash with blood. With every blow he groaned, and I remember wondering how it was possible that no one else could hear him. He glared at me and said, "I do this to protect you." His eyes were wild, and he looked feverish.'

Tilly's trembling and I try to soothe her, but she shies away. 'I screamed at him to stop. I told him I hadn't asked for anything, and certainly not this. We struggled and my hoodie was pulled back, revealing my hair and T-shirt. We staggered about in the water and when he saw me in the wet T-shirt, he turned on me savagely, his eyes ablaze. "Harlot!" he screamed. In one motion, he grabbed me and wrapped a length of the cord from the bundle of branches around my neck. I couldn't breathe, I was terrified, and I flailed against him. He was too strong and slippery with blood from his back. His eyes were closed tight, as he squeezed and squeezed.

'Suddenly, I was in the freezing cold. He'd plunged me into the muddy water and was holding me down. In an instant, I went from choking for breath to drowning. His dark shadow loomed above me, his silhouette fading through the murky water. I grew weaker and tried to scream. A line of bubbles floated to the surface as I begged, "Daddy please…"' She pauses. 'That's when my father killed me.'

I've seen a lot of awful things in my time and heard some terrible stories, but nothing has prepared me for this. For the mind of a warrior to be so utterly deranged that he would destroy the person most precious to him is beyond my understanding. I'm left utterly speechless and can only offer the child the scant comfort of a hug. Inside, my rage is surging, and it is an anger I've felt before, back when my mules were senselessly killed. It is the anger that I fear has sentenced me to an eternity at Brookwood.

I soon realise that the police swarming the cemetery are looking for Callum. It seems they've realised that he's the most likely suspect after Thomas showed them where he thought Callum had been hiding out in the cemetery.

Earlier, the cemetery was deserted, but I find Thomas and Luke gardening again, the radio playing, and Luke humming along. The music is interrupted by a news bulletin. I like to listen to find out what's going on beyond our closed world. The lady talking says something about a mysterious illness that's coming out of China. Thomas doesn't seem particularly worried, but maybe he's just not listening.

My heart is sinking. I've seen this before. I'm straight back with those poor boys arriving in Britain, sick with the influenza off troop trains and ships all the way from Camp Funston, Kansas. We didn't pay it much mind either at first, but it sure took off. In a war-weary world, the flu epidemic of 1918 went on to take a greater toll on humanity than the four preceding years of bloody conflict ever managed to achieve.

I never did understand why they called it Spanish flu, cos I know for sure that it came off the boats from the United States. By the time I got to France, losing my mules and getting myself killed, it was running rife across the country. There are far too many victims who succumbed to it at Brookwood, including our dear Miss Hattie and my friend RSM Torquil McCloud. I can even recall a chilling little song that was popular during that terrible time:

There was a little girl, and she had a little bird.
And she called it by the pretty name of Enza;
But one day it flew away, but it didn't go to stay.
For when she raised the window, in-flu-Enza.

That ditty don't hint at the appalling numbers who died back then, but I saw it with my own eyes. Folks raging with fever and delirium, blood pouring from their noses as their skin turned blue. Eventually, their lungs filled with liquid and they drowned. If this new disease coming out of China is anything like that, may the good Lord help the living, cos they're surely gonna need it.

The radio is calling it Coronavirus or Covid-19. Apparently, it affects old folks more than the young. Back in 1918, it was the youngest and strongest that suffered most. Miss Hattie once explained that although Spanish influenza only had a two-day incubation period, it was so infectious that it penetrated deep into the lungs, causing the body's defences to overreact. The lungs would fill as both the virus and living tissues were attacked. The younger and fitter the victim, the more aggressively the body was tricked into harming itself. That's why many died so tragically young.

Aghast, I leave Luke and his father seemingly oblivious to the danger I fear they will be facing soon. It's been said that, 'As soon as the dying stops, the forgetting begins.' But I'm afraid the world will be remembering pretty darn quick.

Up away in the distance, by the South African plot, I can see some fellers from that time who add a real poignancy to the name of "Brookwood Boys". They're playing an innocent game of football with one of those big old fashioned leather balls. These ain't some local kids showing a singular lack of respect in a cemetery, this is young Tommy Knowles and his South African pals, all killed within a week by the Blue Death, the name they gave to influenza.

The disease didn't discriminate between victims. Across Brookwood there are American boys and nurses, German prisoners of war, boys from Newfoundland, Canada, New Zealand, Australia and all four corners of the British Empire, all laid low. There are officers and battle-scarred veterans, front-line and rear-echelon warriors, all of whom joined fifteen-year-old Tommy and his pals. Civilians, airmen, sailors and soldiers, all treated as equals by the Blue Death.

Tommy's story begins half way around the world. He once told me though, he's spent more years here in England than he ever did alive, but every day he misses the bushveld. Thomas Andrew Knowles was the last of six children born to William and Henrietta in Kimberley, the diamond capital of South Africa. He was the youngest of the brood, indulged as a child, growing into a robust, impetuous boy. Hoping to teach him the British Empire's 'natural order of things', his brother Michael introduced him to the yeomanry regiment of the Kimberley Volunteer Force. It was part-time battalion of weekend warriors and Tommy was by far the youngest trooper, only accepted because he was part of Kimberley's well-respected Knowles family. His troop mates were middle-class white men doing their civic duty and saw Tommy as a lovable scamp, tolerated but in need of discipline.

Ironically, it was Tommy's youth that saved him from the carnage of the Somme offensive. At Delville Wood, the regiment won its first Victoria Cross, but suffered appalling casualties with only 750 survivors from the 3,000 men who entered the wood.

Tales of the glory earnt by the South Africans only goaded Tommy's desire to join them. So in March 1918, still aged only fifteen, Tommy persuaded his father to sign the papers to join the active list. Tommy joined the latest draft embarking at Cape Town onto the HMT *Willochra*, a transport ship destined for England. The great, high-sided ship was far from comfortable and was painted in striking zebra-stripe 'dazzle camouflage' designed to confuse enemy submarines. The Afrikaners onboard dubbed the vessel *die sebra-boot* and soon a carnival-like atmosphere developed during the long trip up the eastern coast of Africa, through the Red Sea, the Suez Canal, then coasting along North Africa through the Mediterranean. It was a happy time for Tommy, who enjoyed the camaraderie, the generous rations, daily gymnastics and games, as well as daily swims in the sea. By the end of the trip, young Tommy and his comrades were in the best shape of their lives, but that's when a few started getting sick.

By 21st of October 1918, Tommy and several of his shipmates were in Woking Military Hospital in Knaphill, Surrey. According to medical records just two days later, young Tommy was dead. On the same day, in that same hospital, ten other South African boys died of what was already being called the 'Blue Death' from dreadful colour of their faces after asphyxiation from fluid-filled lungs. Eight of the dead were on the HMT *Willochra* with Tommy. Tommy is the youngest soldier buried at Brookwood Military Cemetery.

20216 PRIVATE

T.A. KNOWLES

1ST REGT. SOUTH AFRICAN INF.

22ND OCTOBER 1918 AGE 15

CHRIST WILL GATHER IN HIS OWN

TO THE PLACE WHERE HE IS GONE

(VII.A.8)

In the second half of 1918, which from Armistice Day onwards should have been a period of celebration and recovery for a war-weary world, more tombstones appeared at Brookwood than at any other period in its history.

I shudder now to recall the bewildered numbers of souls, including our dear Miss Hattie. Most telling are the headstones where names are crammed together, in unseemly haste, as the bodies piled high and the cemetery struggled to bury them fast enough. Order, dignity, honour and paying due respect has always been at the heart of what Brookwood represents, but it so nearly fell apart during those desperate times. My most fervent prayer for the living world is that they don't have to face the same horror once again.

My dark ponderings are interrupted by Youssef, a nice young feller who was a French sailor during World War Two. He's a devout Muslim and Islamic scholar, and we've had many fine conversations over the years.

Youssef was born in Ceuta, by the legendary Pillars of Hercules and the cool waters of *Mare Nostrum*, just across the sea from the rock of Gibraltar. It was an open city in his childhood, but by the time he was a teenager it had been seized by Franco's Spain and life for his family became difficult. They moved to the port of Casablanca in Morocco, where his love affair with the sea blossomed. Sun-drenched days were spent diving for octopus in clear pools, sailing sky-blue feluccas after darting tuna and flirting with the pretty *Pied-Noir* girls promenading the boulevards.

Fresh-faced and earnest, Youssef was slim and large-eyed with dark curls and a ready smile. His faith was worn loosely, and the blood of Europe and Africa flowed in his veins. Broad-shouldered and tanned from manning the sails, he had the hands and splayed toes of a mariner, his destiny written on the waves. He was sixteen when he joined the *Marine Nationale*, serving as a stoker deep in the fetid bowels of a capital ship. Rich, nourishing food and the continuous toil of shovelling coal put muscle on his bones during voyages around the Horn of Africa and to far-flung French colonies. He saw little of the journey except when he came up for air, envying the gulls as they followed the ship's spume. At journey's end, he would then have the chance to explore the shore. Always a dependable shipmate, he was proud to serve *la mére patrie*, despite being from *la France d'outre-mer* — 'Greater' France.

Tensions with Nazi Germany saw the ship recalled to home waters, just as Blitzkrieg was unleashed across northern France. The *contre-torpilleur*, *Mogador*, slipped past the Pillars of Hercules in May 1940, flashing a semaphore greeting to Gibraltar as they sailed for Oran in French Algeria. Once safely within the harbour walls of the Mers-el-Kébir naval base, the crew listened impotently to the news of the debacle at Dunkirk. North Africans and mainland Frenchmen alike were outraged, especially since the pride of *la Force Navale*, Europe's second largest fleet, including seven battleships, remained untested against the *Kriegsmarine*, moored within Oran's anchorage.

The *Salat al-maghrib*, the evening call to prayer rose through the still air on the 3rd of July 1940. The *muezzin's* chant from the port's minaret was shattered by the sound of wailing sirens. Scrambling barefoot to his post as an anti-aircraft gun loader, Youssef was determined that the Nazis should pay for attacking during holy prayers. A multi-engined aircraft swooped, dropping a magnetic mine at the harbour entrance with a tremendous splash. A raucous cheer rose from the quayside as French fighters engaged the enemy, bringing down one attacker in flames. The cheers turned to dismay with the realisation that the planes were not the *Luftwaffe*, but the Royal Air Force.

Shortly after the attack, British warships lying beyond the horizon, opened fire at a range of sixteen kilometres. Successive salvos hurled great spouts of water into the air amongst the fleet at anchor. Several murderous strikes registered, with the *Dreadnought*-class battleship, *Bretagne*, exploding so violently that her entire crew of nine hundred and seventy-seven went to the bottom. *Provence* and *Dunkerque* were severely damaged, and Youssef's own *Mogador* plus two other destroyers grounded to avoid sinking. A total of one thousand, two hundred and ninety-seven Frenchmen were killed by the British that evening.

Aboard *Mogador*, Youssef and his crewmen surveyed the damage. Thick smoke poured from the ship's rear hull, where an armour-piercing shell had struck, detonating near the depth charge magazine. By some miracle, it had failed to trigger it, or else all aboard would have perished. The ship had her bottom on a sand bank with her propellers knocked out of action, but after emergency repairs, she could be towed to a dry dock where she remained until December, before finally limping to Toulon for reconstruction and a complete refit.

For Youssef and his North African *camarades* the loss of their ship was compounded by the new Vichy administration's instructions that they should all return to their homelands until their fate could be decided. In a final twist of the knife, they were forbidden to sail home, because of the Royal Navy's dominance off Gibraltar and Morocco. Instead, they faced an endless rail journey overland, a distance of a thousand kilometres from Oran to Casablanca, right across Algeria and the breadth of Morocco. They travelled along the Maghrebi line, once the pride of *la France d'outre-mer*, but not for them the luxurious dining and sleeper cars, rather an underpowered locomotive that spewed thick black smoke over the livestock carriages full of parched and sweating matelots.

The journey's end was a mixed blessing. Youssef's joy at seeing his family was tainted by the grim duties awaiting him as a supernumerary Maghrebi sailor. In a Greater France that was seething with anger, recriminations, rumours and political manoeuvring, they were ordered to process fifteen thousand repatriated French servicemen, those evacuated from the beaches of Dunkirk in June. After the fall of France, they'd been invited to stay in England and join *Général* de Gaulle's Free French, but had opted for 'home' instead. Youssef was horrified by the sheer number of well-equipped combatants who'd meekly chosen to give up the fight. As outraged as he was at the cowardly, underhand British attack at Oran, he was even more appalled at what he saw as mass cowardice. How could these *camarades* from the mainland meekly capitulate? Where was their loyalty and pride? What of the vaunted *liberté*, *égalité et fraternité* that had been shoved down their throats as children? Surely, *la lutte continue*, the struggle must go on.

The returning men were sullen and sensitive to any reproach. After a difficult journey in British cargo ships, they arrived foul-tempered and in poor condition. In this atmosphere of humiliation and the outrage over Oran, Vichy port authorities seized the British ships and their crews. This struck Youssef as being beneath France's dignity, since it was the Royal Navy that had rescued these men from Dunkirk, at great risk to themselves, and then provided ships to bring them home. He felt torn, becoming increasingly convinced that he needed to flee Vichy to be on the right side of history.

It was whilst he was on leave at his parents' home that his father tuned the radio to a BBC re-diffusion of *Général* de Gaulle's appeal to Frenchmen on the 18th of June 1940. They only caught the end of the broadcast, but it was enough to get him thinking:

'This war is not limited to the unfortunate territory of our country. This war has not ended with the battle of France. It is a worldwide war. For all the faults, the delays and suffering we have endured, this does not mean that out in the world, the means to one day crush our enemies does not exist. Vanquished today by superior mechanical forces, we will tomorrow overcome them by even more superior mechanical forces. The destiny of the

world is before us. I, Général de Gaulle, here in London, invite the officers and soldiers of France located in British territories or who can reach them, with their weapons or without, to join me here. I invite the engineers and the special workers of the armament industries located in British territories or who can reach them, to contact me. Whatever happens, the flame of the French resistance must not be extinguished, nor shall it ever be extinguished.'

Fine and moving words, but not enough to tip him over the edge. It was witnessing Vichy's treatment of innocent civilians that did it. Before the fall of France, the authorities on British Gibraltar had decided that civilians were at risk given the strategic importance of 'The Rock.' Consequently, thirteen and a half thousand civilians were evacuated to the 'safety' of French Morocco. However, when France fell, they unexpectedly found themselves stranded in what was now enemy territory. Youssef and his *camarades* were tasked with guarding these refugees, amongst whom were several members of his extended family. They were being kept in appalling conditions and treated with disproportionate cruelty, in spite of having nothing to do with the Oran attack.

Their presence was also an embarrassment to Vichy, keen not to offend the German occupiers of mainland France. The authorities decided that the Gibraltarian refugees must leave French Morocco within twenty-four hours and would be returned in the impounded British cargo ships. The commodore leading this flotilla objected vehemently, saying his vessels were unsuitable for the transport of women and children. He was overruled and the terrified refugees were forced aboard with rifle butts wielded by Vichy troops on the quayside.

Seeing such innocents being brutalised appalled Youssef. After all, Gibraltar was named for *Jabal-al-Tariq*, the Mountain of Tariq, after the Moorish leader who established Islam in Europe. Familiar faces beseeched him for help, as children wailed and women fainted in the blazing heat. A pregnant woman collapsed, spurring Youssef into action. Handing his rifle to a *camarade*, he swept her up in his arms and barged his way up the gangplank. In his naval uniform, no one hampered his progress, and he was able to get Jane, his pale ward, to settle and dry her tears. He left her in the care of her family, who he'd also hustled aboard.

This was the point when Youssef made the decision that would change the direction of his life. He chose to stay aboard and join the fight in England. Stowing away wasn't difficult for an experienced mariner like him. Once the ship was underway, he presented himself to a naval ensign and was questioned by the Officer of the Watch. His good English, picked up on his travels, certainly helped convince him and since none of the English sailors spoke much French, he proved to be a very useful stowaway. At first he was held as an 'enemy combatant', but after a few hours he was released and immediately taken under the wing of Jane's family. She was with her parents Nigel and Josefina, her two sisters and her gruff old Uncle Tobias, a former Royal Marine who had married into the Gibraltarian family. Initially suspicious of the 'Frog', Uncle Tobias changed his opinion when Youssef shared his plans to join the Free French.

'I'll sort you out, my lad,' he promised. 'Still got some clout in this navy. Once we're back in Blighty, we'll have a pint and I'll get you fixed up. You're a bit skinny for a marine, but the navy can always use a good man.'

'*Merci, monsieur*,' replied Youssef. 'I'll look for the Free French Navy in *Angleterre*.'

'Don't you worry, my son. They'll be pleased to have you. Now, how about you find us some more water for Janie and the girls?'

Youssef nodded.

'There's a good lad. I'll stay here and watch over things,' he said, waving the stem of his pipe. This soon became the established routine of the vomit-inducing voyage to England. The ship zigzagged across the Atlantic, avoiding U-boats and crashing through waves that threatened to swamp the chugging old rust bucket. With the iron stomach of a veteran sailor, Youssef found himself nursing the whole family, especially *Madame* Jane, who seemed to get sicker and sicker from the *mal de mer*. Even the redoubtable *Oncle* Toby eventually succumbed, mercifully putting a stop to his evil-smelling pipe, which had triggered much of his family's nausea.

After sixteen exhausting days, the ragged convoy reached the port of the recently bombed Bristol. They were followed in by herring gulls, who shrieked malevolently, giving Youssef the *al-'ayn*, the evil eye. He rubbed the *nazar* amulet he kept on a string around his neck to ward off their spell.

The docks were in worse shape than even those he'd left at Oran. Blackened warehouses on the wharves loomed through the grey drizzle, with collapsed metal cranes lying like the skeletons of sea creatures, their heads in the water and ribbed bodies splayed on the quayside. The weary dockers on them looked tired, grimy and in a state of shock. The Blitz had clearly hit the city hard.

The evacuees from Gibraltar were bound for London, where they would most likely face the even greater threat of the London Blitz. True to his word, Uncle Toby bought Youssef a pint at the first pub they found and accompanied him to the Royal Marines recruiting office. The sergeant in charge was happy to make enquiries, and it emerged that the headquarters of the Free French Naval Forces was also in London at Stafford Mansions, SW1, near Buckingham Palace. Youssef would therefore join the family in crossing this strange, permanently wet and tired war-torn country.

They had an emotional farewell at Paddington station. Youssef then faced what for a young Maghrebi country-boy was a terrifying but exhilarating ordeal: his very first journey on the underground. The thought of travelling *under* the great city was inconceivable to him and made him feel queasy, something the mighty Atlantic had singularly failed to do.

By the time he was interviewed by an immaculately dressed Naval ensign at Stafford Mansions, he was recovered, but felt embarrassed at the state of his own uniform. He needn't have worried; the officer congratulated him on his patriotism and thanked him for volunteering. Youssef was provided with requisition forms for a new uniform, a ration book full of coupons for food and refreshments, and an accommodation chit for the Royal Automobile Club in London's Pall Mall, home of the Free French Forces in London.

By day's end, he was kitted out and had a four-day *permission* to visit London. He would then receive fresh orders to join the ship's company of the *Chacal*-class destroyer, *FFL Léopard*, refitting in Portsmouth. The vessel was commanded by *Lieutenant de Vaisseau* Jules Evenou, who's *nom de guerre* was Jacques Richard, to protect his family in France. Youssef wondered whether he would need one. The ship was due to depart for the Clyde in Scotland within weeks, tasked with anti-submarine duties to protect vital Atlantic convoys that came in and out of the Clyde via the North-Western Approaches.

FFL Léopard's first mission was escorting eleven merchant ships that had been delayed by fog to a rendezvous point with

Convoy WS5B, a 'Winston Special' destined for Freetown, Sierra Leone. Departing on the 12th of January 1941, they then returned to Clyde two days later in the company of the British destroyer HMS *Witherington*. Youssef was delighted to be back at sea, but once again found the mid-Atlantic waves terrifying when compared to the friendly seas of his Mediterranean youth. Towering slabs of dark water loomed over them for much of the journey, while gale force winds howled. Serving on deck, he was permanently soaked and freezing, but was moved by the sight of the red *Croix de Lorraine* on the tricolour, flapping to shreds but proudly declaring that France was in the fight.

Returning to port, battered and bruised, Youssef discovered that FFL *Léopard* would be back on duty within days, to escort a troopship destined for Canada. These short voyages, shepherding their unarmed charges through the coastal waters, were vital as they were at the mercy of the *Kriegsmarine's* wolf-packs, but the trips soon became routine. On 24th February, FFL *Léopard* rescued forty-one survivors of the merchant ship, SS *Waynegate*, from the icy waters. Part of Convoy OB-288, she'd been sunk by torpedoes from U-73, south of Iceland in the early hours of the morning. The ship's master had ordered the crew to abandon ship, and not long afterwards the U-boat surfaced to deliver the *coup de grâce* to the listing hulk. Two lifeboats filled with the ship's terrified crew were so close that they were almost struck by a flying metal plate from the exploding ship. Their attacker then slipped silently below the waves, abandoning them to their fate.

The next six days were spent adrift on the bitterly cold Icelandic Sea, until they were finally rescued by *FFL Léopard*. Struck dumb with hypothermia, the ship's master, his crew of thirty-eight and two Royal Navy gunners moved like centenarians, as Youssef helped them aboard. None could string together a sentence, even after hours spent under warm rugs, drinking sugary rum-spiked tea. Youssef thanked his merciful God for the opportunity to have come to the rescue of these unfortunates.

FFL Léopard was an old ship, launched at St. Nazaire in 1924. She leaked fuel and had a troublesome boiler and a smoky first stack. Returning homewards with Convoy WS7, she was sent to the Kingston upon Hull naval yard in east Yorkshire for a refit and repairs. Her boiler and faulty funnel were replaced, oil storage tanks were added, and her aged depth charge chutes were updated. She was now equipped with six dozen Mk VIIH heavy (251 Kg) depth charges and two dozen Mk VII (191 Kg) ones. Her old guns and aft torpedo tubes were replaced by three 20 mm Oerlikon AA guns, a pair of quad Vickers half-inch guns and a Type 291 search radar. All of which was too technical for Youssef but gave him the opportunity to re-train for a new role. He would now man one of the four new Thornycroft depth charge throwers on deck, taking the battle to the enemy below the waves. He would also be exposed to the worst of the elements, handling heavy equipment on the slippery deck.

Once seaworthy again, *FFL Léopard* was tasked with escorting Convoy OS33, bound for Freetown on 11th July 1942. Off the coast of Madeira, the enemy submarine U-136 was sighted on the surface by HMS *Spey*, which set off in pursuit. She fired a pattern of depth charges, followed by a spread of contact-firing spigot mortar bombs from a new Hedgehog anti-submarine projector and managed to wing the enemy, slowing them down. This gave *FFL Léopard* time to set up her own depth charges and fire a pattern over the side.

Detonating at pre-set depths, the booms deep underwater threw plumes of white water into the air. FFL *Léopard* criss-crossed the position, launching several more lines of the barrel-shaped charges, each projected forty metres out and designed to fall through the icy waters before exploding.

The second line fired brought up foam fouled with black oil, marking the destruction of U-136, lost with all forty-five hands, including *Kapitänleutnant* Heinrich Zimmerman, aged thirty-five. He'd been responsible for sinking five merchant ships and two warships during his three-tour career. Youssef took no pleasure in the killing of these men but knew they had been responsible for many deaths. Today it was just their turn to lose. *Inshallah*. Whilst he was securing the unused charges back in their racks, he wondered when it might be his turn to die.

The next day, as FFL *Léopard* manoeuvred through rough seas, she collided with Grimsby-class Royal Navy sloop HMS *Lowestoft*. FFL *Léopard*'s bow was stove in with such a powerful jolt that a line of depth-charges were released from their rack. Rolling across the deck, the dead weight of one rolled into *Matelot breveté* Youssef Alaoui, crushing his chest and pinning him against the rack.

The ship limped into Gibraltar five days later, but Youssef never regained consciousness, nor did he realise just how close to home he was. Re-embarked onto the British hospital ship, HMHS *Chantilly*, bound for England, Youssef Alaoui died of his wounds on the day the ship reached Portsmouth. He was back in England, and this time it was for good. He was buried in Brookwood's Free French plot under these few words:

YOUSSEF ALAOUI

MARIN FNFL

19.8.1942

Youssef is a very kind, gentle and reflective young man who sacrificed his life for France. At Brookwood, he leads a prayer group amongst the many servicemen from India, what is now Bangladesh and Pakistan, North Africa, Iraq, Iran and Egypt. All these men fought and died bravely for the British Empire during some war or another.

Over the years, it has saddened Youssef to see his faith harden, leading to conflict with all others when it had coexisted for centuries. I know he's horrified that most of the modern casualties joining us, young men like Mack, were killed whilst fighting against fellow Muslims around the world. I've seen him in tears, asking, 'How can we be such hate-filled enemies? What has created this hatred, where there was once brotherly love?'

I have no answer, but together we've watched the conflicts in Iraq and Afghanistan reach their twentieth year and spread to Syria, Libya and elsewhere. It appears that man has singularly failed to learn the lessons that we who lie here have learnt all too well.

Youssef has two members of his prayer group with him. Like me, they enjoy the dawn and hold their prayer meetings at sun-up. Normally so serene a character, this morning Youssef seems anxious.

'*Sergent* Mouse,' he says. 'We have found something worrying that you should know about. You know we hold our dawn prayers every morning. As we have no minaret for the call to prayer, we like to climb high to be nearer to God. We use the roof of one of the Persian mausolea, on the hillside beyond the military plots.'

I'm wondering what he's getting at.

'This morning, I began the call of *Salat al-fajr* across the cemetery, to thank Allah, glorified and exalted, for bringing us another beautiful sunrise. Over on the other side of the valley, there was a large bald man on top of another sepulchre. He was not one of us. He was of the living and dressed like a soldier, but also prayed barefoot on his prayer mat. *How strange*, I thought, *for one of the living to be in the cemetery so very early.* That's when the sun glinted on something he was holding in his arms. It was a gun.'

I catch my breath. It can only be Tilly's daddy, Callum.

'Where is this man now?' I ask, immediately concerned. My mind is racing, and I'm grateful that Brookwood still seems deserted this early on a Sunday morning.

The Long Avenue runs along the southern perimeter of Brookwood Military Cemetery, parallel to the culvert where we found poor Tilly. It continues into the main civilian cemetery, running past the Czech plot where Miroslav Ludek and his June are buried.

The Giant Redwoods lining the avenue were planted over two hundred years ago, predating all the military dead in our cemetery. Other trees have been planted since, Canadian Maples and Lebanese Cedars, to symbolise everlasting life, but it is the giant red pines that are most famously associated with Brookwood. Each specimen is well over two hundred feet tall, broad at the base with deceptively large, bowed branches high up in the canopy. The upper reaches of the trees are barely visible and hard to make out as they are screened by thick green boughs and branches growing in every direction. Visitors are often impressed by the girth of the trunks and surprised by the spongy softness of the thick fissured bark. The sheer size of these trees is hard to take in, but observers rarely look up into the high canopy, where many creatures live and thrive.

They would never suspect that there is a man up there, hidden amongst the swaying branches and dark shadows.

I glance around to see if more living visitors have arrived and am relieved to see the grounds are still quite deserted. It's early, though, and the place is bound to get busier since it's a Sunday. From his position, Tilly's daddy has a better view of the cemetery than me.

News has got around and I can see my anxious comrades approaching. Taddy and Miss Hattie are with Bill and Louis. Behind them, hand in hand are a pale-faced Tilly and her Mack. Rather self-consciously following the group are Lee and Willy. Whatever the outcome of today, it seems there will be an audience.

I go straight up to Lee. I'd sent word that I wanted to see him in particular. 'Thanks for coming. I surely do appreciate it. Lee, we're gonna need your skill to climb up that monster. I've seen you do it plenty of times, but wonder whether you might teach me how? Maybe you'd come up with me too?'

'Yes, sir, I reckon I could. Been up them before; it ain't so hard for them that know how. Their soft bark helps, but the most important thing to remember is that there's nothing to fear from the tree.' He steps up and touches the red bark, almost as if he's communicating with it. Lee then looks straight up the seemingly endless trunk. 'Don't fear the height, nor the possibility of slipping or falling, since none of that can harm you. It is only your mind that can, Mouse, so it is the fear within that must be ignored.'

I look into the earnest eyes of this man who for so long has refused to repent his crimes, but is now offering to help. He still stinks of cigarettes and the fluids that escaped him as he kicked his life away at the end of Pierrepoint's rope. None of that is important now; we need his expertise if we are to avert a disaster that would surely damn Brookwood's name forever.

Lee takes me by the hand and leads me to the base of the tall pine, peering up the fissured trunk to the lofty canopy. I can't help but feel intimidated by the tree's size.

'It's only fear that holds you back, Mouse,' whispers Lee in his rope-burned hiss. 'Our hands and feet can't actually interact with the surface of the bark, so it is only our will that allows us to climb. I can make progress, but only by willing myself upwards.' He looks up again and turns to me. 'You'll see, Sergeant Mouse, it's as easy as it looks. Just believe and follow my example. Don't think on the height and in no time, we'll be right up there with him.'

He nods respectfully to Miss Hattie, who smiles at him, then pats old Willy on the shoulder, who links his hands into a stirrup to give Lee a leg up. Reaching above his head height, he places his hand upon the red bark. He raises his right foot above the level of his other knee, appearing to kick his toe into the tree trunk. He starts to climb, hauling himself upwards, and is soon making steady progress up the giant tree.

I take a deep breath, close my eyes and reach up like he did. I feel myself sliding upwards, my feet mimicking the actions Lee has demonstrated. By the time I have the courage to open my eyes, he's fifty feet above me, climbing steadily, and I'm making good progress too. It takes a while to get up there, but I concentrate on my actions to override my fear and the exertion of the climb. Things get easier once we reach Callum's ropes and the tangled spread of branches higher up. Getting closer, his silhouette becomes more distinct, and I can hear various bits of equipment clinking in the breeze. Lee is almost at his height now, and I'm about fifteen feet below when I stop to examine what I can see of him.

He's wearing what I can only call a 'hairy' suit, blending in perfectly with the tree's bark and foliage. I can't see his face, as it's hidden by a hood, but I can hear him reciting something over and over again. There's the smell of alcohol on the breeze as he reaches into his pocket and takes a long pull from a silver flask, shiny amid his camouflage.

'He can see for miles from up there,' says Lee. The combination of odours — urine, faeces, tobacco and whisky — coming off the pair is nauseating and I'm grateful that the breeze is picking up. I look around and my heart lurches as I realise the cemetery is filling with visitors and the carpark is half full. Above my head, I hear a chuckle from within the hood.

'Aha, my old pal Thomas, I see you're back again.' Callum's voice is surprisingly deep. The black nose of his rifle moves as he tracks something on the ground. 'We all suffer in war, don't we, old pal? It's just that some of us have lost more than others. We who have stood on the wall, defending the weak, are called to sacrifice the most, but are abandoned when we fall. These sheep don't deserve our sacrifice. We did our duty, what we had to. It's cost me everything: my mind, my wife, my daughter. Maybe it's your turn to pay too, old pal.'

I scan the horizon and spot two familiar figures standing side by side. With a jolt, I realise it's Thomas and Luke, Callum's first intended targets. He shifts as he aims and his hood parts just enough for me to see his pale eye peering into the sniper scope. I'm too far away to reach him, even if I could divert him from his chilling purpose.

I call up to Lee, who is closer to Callum. 'Lee, for the love of God do something! He's going to shoot the boy!'

I cannot fathom how Lee does it, but it looks like he takes a cigarette from his lips, reaches over and just pokes it straight into Callum's eye. Callum gives a high-pitched shriek and starts clawing at his face. It's all a scrambling blur, then suddenly something heavy is falling. A long, frustrated scream is abruptly cut off. The rope running down the trunk tightens, then slaps viciously as a lumpen mass is jerking at its end.

Unveiled as he falls, Callum's face is staring up at me. His neck is at an unnatural angle, the bright red rope wrapped around it. His lifeless eyes are the same colour as Tilly's, but his head is bald, the scalp, chin and eyebrows all shaved clean. The iris of his left eye and the eyelid bear the vivid red mark of whatever Lee managed to poke into it. Below us, there is a clatter that shakes me from my shocked reverie. It's Callum's sniper rifle, hitting the roots at the base of the tree.

'How on earth did you do that?' I ask Lee.

'I dunno,' he replies. 'Sometimes I dream of being back at Shepton Mallet, where I got hanged. I see them people poking about where I spent my final moments and that gets me angry. They show me no respect, so I burn them. I don't know exactly how I do it. What I saw got me real mad, that this man wants to hurt people. I had to do something. I saw his eye, so I burnt it.'

Far below us, our comrades are clustered around the base of the tree. Amongst them, I see Tilly sobbing and being comforted by Mack and Miss Hattie. It is a terrible sound to hear rising up through the boughs of the giant tree. It's the wail of yet another child grieving a lost parent, and sadly a sound that is all too familiar at Brookwood. It all seems such a terrible, wasteful tragedy.

EPILOGUE

March, 2020

The grounds are deserted these days. Once in a while, I catch a glimpse of Thomas, checking the chains on the gates. At least, I think it's Thomas, since his face is hidden behind a blue face mask. No work is happening on the bulbs or flowering plants, none of the mowing of grass that would normally be taking place at this time of year.

With no visitors and no gardeners working, it's hard for me to be sure of what's actually happening in the wider world. The mask tells me that Coronavirus has spread to these shores, but we've not seen any surge in burials within the military cemetery, so that's an encouraging sign. I'm told there is more activity than usual over in Brookwood's civilian cemetery, and from their high vantage point, I know Youssef and his prayer group have seen and heard many Islamic funerals. Their sense is that the death toll is rising and the Shrieker in the trees seems to agree, providing a haunting cacophony as out there in the real world, a deadly turmoil is brewing.

For our part, in a world that sees so little change, there has been a good deal lately. The loneliness that plagued me is dissipating, and I don't underestimate Tilly's role in that. She and Mack have moved on now, which makes me a little sad, but I'm glad they've found peace. The tragedy of her young life cut short was offset by the joy she experienced with Mack.

Before she and Mack disappeared, Tilly came to me with a gift. Fully restored by now, she was almost radiant in death. Smiling sweetly, she took my big old hands in hers. 'My darling

Mouse, I've got something to tell you.' She was looking straight at me with those dazzling green eyes of hers. 'I can't keep calling you Mouse.' I frowned, puzzled at the expression on her face. With a little giggle, she said, 'How about Grandpa?'

I was mighty confused. She went on to explain that she believed she was my great-great-great granddaughter. It appears her grandmother, Lillian, had a grandmother called Nan-nan, short for Nancy. Now, would you believe that Nancy was my own little Nancy from Winchester? It's all a bit complicated for an old-timer like me but Tilly told me she had genetic proof from the analysis of her saliva. The results said her blood contained African ancestry, but also Native American. I was finding all this kinda hard to believe, but that was what really threw me. You see, I never did tell nobody that old Uncle Red was part Chickasaw. Seeing as he was my daddy's full brother, well, I surely must be too.

My darling little Nancy, who I've dreamt of so often, was actually the mother of my child. That was the news she'd been so desperate to tell me before I left for France. She had — no, rather *we* had a little daughter called Florence. I'd always had a hankering for a family, and now I had Tilly, my four-times granddaughter. I've come to realise she always did have Nancy's beautiful eyes and that sad, haunting smile.

The time we spent together was more joyful than any ghost might expect to be. It was a shock when she moved on, but I accepted that her and Mack's time had come.

I know mine will come too, but in the meantime, I have others to care for. Tilly's daddy, Callum, is here with us and still has his problems. It'll take time for him to heal, time for forgiveness and understanding to grow, but hell, we've got nothing but time. I owe it to him, being kin and all, to see him right, for in all this, surely he's a victim too. So, with Taddy and the rest of my broken little gang of spirits, we'll fix him and fix each other and by and by our time will surely come. In the meantime, we wait and watch as the world endures once more.

It is the wise old head on Youssef's young shoulders that said, '*Plus ça change, plus c'est la même chose.* The more things change, the more they stay the same.' Well, I don't know about that, but I guess for now, that'll have to do.

A NOTE TO THE READER

Dear Reader,

The inspiration for this story came to me during the second Coronavirus lockdown here in Great Britain. At the time, my family and I lived near Woking, Surrey (*A Town called Malice* for fans of Paul Weller and The Jam), and Brookwood Cemetery was a quiet place with not too many people where I could walk and get some much-needed fresh air and a change of ideas.

I've always had an interest in history, military history in particular, and a penchant for visiting cemeteries and graveyards. Europe has many of the former, given its turbulent history, and it has been a longtime habit of mine to visit military cemeteries and memorials across several countries to pay my respects.

In this respect, Woking is well served. On outskirts of the town, linked to London by the railway, is Brookwood Military Cemetery, the largest in the United Kingdom. It is itself within Brookwood Cemetery, which was once the largest cemetery in Western Europe. I believe it may since have been superseded by Our Lady of Almudena Cemetery in Madrid, Spain. Suffice to say Brookwood, also known as the London Necropolis, was initially created to house all of the capital's dead and is absolutely vast, very atmospheric, a little run down and frankly rather spooky.

In contrast, and as might be expected, the military cemetery is immaculate, with rows upon rows of gravestones, principally of the standard Commonwealth War Graves Commission shape for British and Commonwealth servicemen, but also with marble crosses for Americans, and other shaped stones for the French, German, Belgian, Czech, Polish, Italian and soldiers of many other nations that lie here. There are also some differently shaped tombstones for the Islamic and Jewish faiths. That is before even mentioning the huge diversity of sepulchres, mausolea and funerary monuments, both grand and modest that are spread across the many acres of the vast 'civilian' cemetery.

What is particularly striking about the Brookwood is the sheer diversity of nations, faiths and indeed the different conflicts that have claimed the lives of these many soldiers. The largest contingents are from the First and particularly the Second World War, but there has been a tragically consistent influx ever since then.

When beginning my research into the many stories of the soldiers buried here, I was struck by how many secrets, untold stories, misinformation and subterfuge are hidden behind the mute lanes of engraved stone and the monuments to the lost. I refer in my story to the disaster at Slapton Sands in Devon before D-Day, the most murderous of V-1 Doodlebug attacks on London, and indeed others, whose many victims lie or did lie buried at Brookwood. Also, of the executed murderers and rapists of the US Armed Forces buried here for a while, but then transferred away for 'dishonourable burial' in France along with all the others similarly guilty of heinous crimes against civilians or their brother soldiers and executed across the European theatre of operations. That such a disproportionate number of them should be of African American or of non-White origin is deeply troubling and indicative of the institutional racism of the time which it is difficult to conceive today.

I found the transporting around of the remains of the dead, often surreptitiously at night, after the Slapton Sands disaster and certain V-1 explosions puzzling. Also, the removal of all WWII American dead from Brookwood after the war to either the centralised Cambridge American Cemetery or being repatriated to the United States also somewhat perplexing. Not least, because why then would they leave the American WWI burials behind? This may or may not have been a way of 'confusing' the trail of where certain bodies came from, but also created the scenario where the area which had previously held the WWII American dead was now reused to inter the remains of Italian servicemen, predominantly Prisoners of War, and also the Free French plot. The potential 'turf wars' that might occur between 'spirits' all claiming the same acreage was something interesting for me to consider.

You may have noted that I have dotted the text of my story with the inscriptions of several gravestones. I hope you find that provides a flavour of what walking through the cemetery feels like. As might be expected, some of the inscriptions relate to fictional characters, which I have invented, but some are composites of real people, others still are actually buried at Brookwood. Should anyone be interested and if you ever find your way to visiting Brookwood Military Cemetery you could spend some time paying your respects to some of those lying beneath the tombstones detailed. Those listed with numbers and letters in brackets, can be found by their plot number and position. Mouse's marble cross, inscribed with the words: *HERE RESTS IN HONORED GLORY, AN AMERICAN SOLDIER KNOWN BUT TO GOD,* might be any of the forty-three graves of WWI unknown warriors that are situated before the American Memorial Chapel.

This story is ultimately about the legacy that war leaves behind, mentally, physically and how the trace of it reaches far down into our living memory. I hope you have found it thought-provoking, perhaps a little challenging and that some of the themes may remain in your thoughts for a while. I think they deserve to, don't you?

A final snippet that I will leave with you, actually provided the inspiration as to how one of the final scenes of the story might be resolved. Following is a real extract of a newspaper article that appeared in *The Sun* newspaper in 2017. Granted, it is a somewhat sensationalist tabloid publication, but at the time had the highest circulation of any newspaper in Great Britain.

GHOST 'ATTACK'

Prison tour guide claims he was BURNED by ghost of executed murderer inside the UK's most haunted nick. *He said the experience has definitely caused him a few sleepless nights and now he always locks up the prison at night with a colleague.*

A PRISON tour guide is convinced he was burned by the GHOST of an executed murderer.

Paul Toole, 42, felt a searing pain on his hand while showing a group of visitors round Shepton Mallet Prison. He later found he had a cigarette burn - now tour guides refuse to lock up the building alone.

Paul, from Wells, Somerset, was telling the story of chain-smoking Private Lee Davis, a former inmate who was executed for rape and murder and refused to accept his fate before he was hanged. Paul said: 'As part of the tour we show the visitors the condemned man's cells. Originally there would have been a bookcase hiding the doorway from the cell through to the execution room, which is where I was stood when I was telling the story of the inmate, Lee Davis. I had done a little research about the prison in the days leading up to the tour and it had been the very first time I had ever told this story to the visitors. As I was talking, I felt this very sharp pain but tried to ignore it while I was stood in front of the visitors. When I looked down at it later it looked like a cigarette burn.'

Paul had researched a former inmate, who was executed at the prison in December 1943 for the murder of Cynthia Lay and the rape of her friend, Muriel Fawden, despite inconsistencies in the evidence. It was claimed that Davis could not accept his fate and as he was led to the gallows shouted, 'Oh my God, I'm going to die.'

Paul said the experience has definitely caused him a few sleepless nights and now he always locks up the prison at night with a colleague. He said: 'I'm quite a sensitive person but I always lock up the prison with someone else since it happened. People probably think I'm a bit crackers but there is so much that goes on in the prison. Lights go on and off, you can hear doors banging and areas of prison will get really cold all of a sudden.

The prison is renowned for ghostly goings on, and it is believed a woman in white, who died of a broken heart in 1680 after murdering her fiancée, wanders the empty corridors between wings A and B. When the building still operated as a prison, there are tales of officers refusing to work night shifts for fear of seeing a deathly figure wandering the corridors.

Shepton Mallet was one of the oldest working prisons in the UK, as well as the highest walled prison and many of the executed inmates are buried in unmarked graves in the grounds. The prison also housed many notorious criminals such as the Kray twins, after they refused to take part in national service in 1952.

Paul said: 'The prison has a fascinating history, but it will soon be turned into apartments. It has a special place in my heart because it's such an amazing historical site and it's such a shame it can't be protected.'

Fans of the supernatural can spend the night in Somerset's Shepton Mallet Prison, and even have a go at hunting some of the ghosts that call the prison their home.

I hope you've enjoyed reading *The Brookwood Boys*. It would be great if you would post a review on **Amazon** or **Goodreads**. Readers can also connect with me on **Twitter (@P33ddy)** and via **my website**. Also, for anyone who may be interested, I have loaded some images on **Instagram (brookwood.boys)** that inspired me to write the story of Mouse and his family of spirits.

Best regards,
Patrick Larsimont
October 2024

patricklarsimont.com

Sapere Books is an exciting new publisher of brilliant fiction and popular history.

To find out more about our latest releases and our monthly bargain books visit our website:
saperebooks.com

www.ingramcontent.com/pod-product-compliance
Lightning Source LLC
Chambersburg PA
CBHW060440180626
46817CB00007B/2912